MURDER ON THE FRENCH RIVIERA

A LADY ELIZABETH HAWTHORNE MYSTERY

OLIVIA ROSE

Copyright © 2024 by Olivia Rose

All rights reserved.

No part of this publication may be reproduced, distributed, or transmitted in any form or by any means, including photocopying, recording, or other electronic or mechanical methods, without the prior written permission of the publisher, except as permitted by U.S. copyright law. For permission requests, contact [include publisher/author contact info].

The story, all names, characters, and incidents portrayed in this production are fictitious. No identification with actual persons (living or deceased), places, buildings, and products is intended or should be inferred.

Publisher: Olivia Rose

Editor: Trish Long (Blossoming Pages Services)

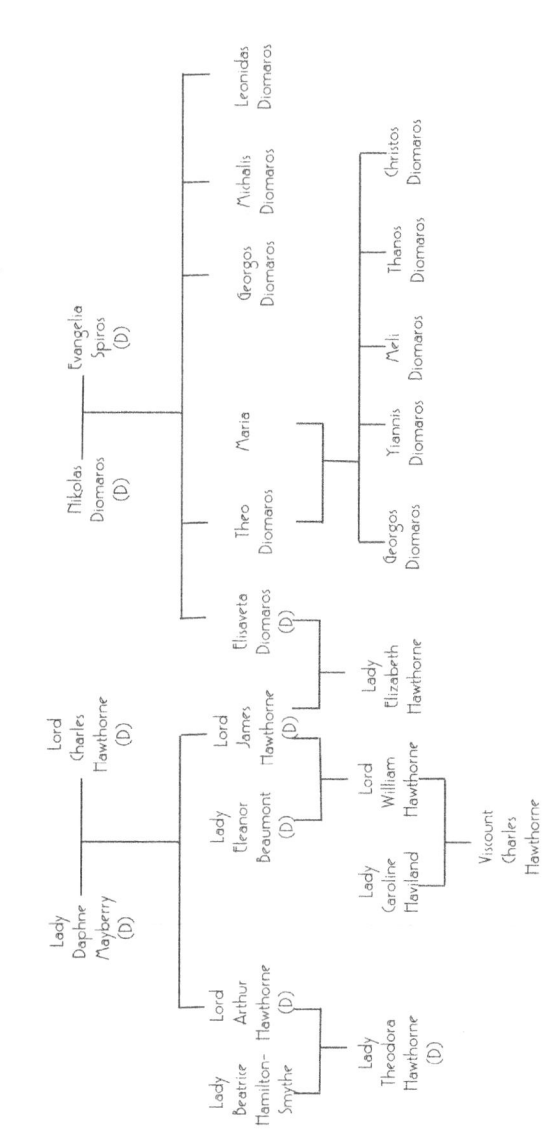

Lady Elizabeth Hawthorne - Family Tree

Hawthorne Side

Lady Daphne Mayberry (D) — **Lord Charles Hawthorne (D)**

Children:
- Lord Arthur Hawthorne (D) — Lady Beatrice Hamilton-Smythe
  - Lady Theodora Hawthorne (D)
- Lady Eleanor Beaumont (D) — Lord James Hawthorne (D)
  - Lord William Hawthorne — Lady Caroline Hayland
    - Viscount Charles Hawthorne
  - Lady Elizabeth Hawthorne — Elisaveta Diomaros (D)

Diomaros Side

Nikolas Diomaros (D) — **Evangelia Spiros (D)**

Children:
- Theo Diomaros
- Maria
- Georgos Diomaros
- Michalis Diomaros
- Leonidas Diomaros

Children of Theo and Maria:
- Georgos Diomaros
- Yiannis Diomaros
- Meli Diomaros
- Thanos Diomaros
- Christos Diomaros

Contents

Chapter One	1
Chapter Two	15
Chapter Three	34
Chapter Four	53
Chapter Five	68
Chapter Six	87
Chapter Seven	106
Chapter Eight	118
Chapter Nine	130
Chapter Ten	143
Chapter Eleven	162
Chapter Twelve	174
Chapter Thirteen	191
Chapter Fourteen	204

Chapter Fifteen	218
Chapter Sixteen	230
Chapter Seventeen	245
Chapter Eighteen	265
Chapter Nineteen	279
Chapter Twenty	290
Chapter Twenty-One	307
Chapter Twenty-Two	316
Epilogue	322
Dedication	329
Also by Olivia Rose	330
About the Author	335

Chapter One

THE WHISTLE OF *Le Train Bleu* reverberated sharply through the *Gare de Cannes* as Lady Elizabeth Hawthorne and her entourage disembarked onto the bustling platform. Accompanied by her cousin Meli, Aunt Beatrice, and Evelyn, Aunt Beatrice's lady's companion, Elizabeth stepped from the train into a world transformed. They had travelled from the brisk, frosty air of Calais, across the breathtaking, snow-draped peaks of the French Alps, and through the verdant stretches of Provence. Now, their journey culminated in the warmth of the French Riviera. The salty whispers of the nearby sea mingled with the delicate, fruity essence of winter honeysuckle and the heady sweetness of mimosa blossoms – the golden heralds of this sun-drenched coastal enclave favoured by Europe's elite and wealthy.

Elizabeth tightened her rose-coloured jacket, its tailored silhouette skimming her waist as she braced against the brisk sea breeze skimming across the platform. Her sleek, ink-dark bob peeked out from beneath the brim of her stylish cloche hat, framing her hazel eyes.

Beside her, Meli practically vibrated with palpable excitement, her every gesture brimming with energy that seemed to mirror the bustling activity of the train station. The bold pattern of her emerald dress caught the light as she turned, her toffee-coloured eyes sparkling with excitement. 'Oh, Elizabeth, can you believe we're finally here?' Her hands gestured animatedly, her enthusiasm infectious as her words bubbled with unrestrained delight.

Cutting through the lively chatter, the authoritative presence of Aunt Beatrice emerged from the crowd, her silver-grey hair swept up in an impeccable chignon that accentuated the regal line of her jaw. The high collar of her dark velvet gown added to the austere elegance of her bearing, while the sapphire hue of her eyes surveyed the scene with a critical gaze. Evelyn, ever the dutiful companion, moved in sync with Aunt Beatrice, her chestnut curls neatly pinned back and her expression one of quiet, unwavering composure, despite the gentle bustle around them.

"Honestly, Evelyn, must you dawdle?" Aunt Beatrice's clipped tone, laced with impatience, sliced through the ambient noise as she forged a path ahead, her dark velvet gown swishing with each purposeful stride.

A flicker of strain crossed Evelyn's features, a subtle crack in her otherwise composed demeanour, before she recomposed herself. "Forgive me, Lady Hawthorne," she responded, her voice soft yet assured.

Elizabeth's heart clenched as Evelyn's composure wavered, a flicker of strain crossing her features. Aunt Beatrice's sharp reprimand, though familiar, still stung to witness.

Elizabeth glanced at Aunt Beatrice, then back at Evelyn. She reached out and brushed her fingers against Evelyn's arm in a gesture of support.

Evelyn's eyes briefly met Elizabeth's, a forced smile tightening her lips. She took a subtle, deep breath, her shoulders tensing under the fabric of her coat. As she exhaled, the tension in her expression eased, her features rearranging themselves into the familiar mask she presented to the world.

As the last hiss of steam evaporated into the air, porters sprang into action, shuttling luggage from the train to the line of gleaming motorcars. Meli, struggling to contain her excitement, hopped from one foot to the other, her eyes bright with anticipation. "Can you believe it, Elizabeth? We're actually here!"

Amid the organised chaos, Aunt Beatrice stood with an air of imperious patience, her gaze sweeping over the scene. She turned to Elizabeth. "Where on earth is our car?" she demanded, her voice cutting through the hum of the bustling platform.

Quick to soothe, Elizabeth took her aunt's elbow, directing her gaze towards a Rolls Royce Silver Ghost parked nearby. The motorcar's dark grey exterior shimmered under the pale winter sun, its chrome accents catching the light with a dazzling sparkle. "It's there, Aunt," Elizabeth assured her, her voice calm and reassuring. As her aunt's eyes followed the gesture, the tension in her shoulders visibly eased.

Victor, resplendent in the maroon and gold livery of Le Majestique Palais de Cannes, stood at attention beside the gleaming Rolls Royce. As the ladies approached, he acknowledged their arrival with a crisp nod, the corners of his dark eyes crinkling as a warm smile spread across his face.

"Lady Hawthorne, welcome back!" His words carried a crisp, clear French accent, echoing the warmth of the Riviera sun.

Elizabeth's eyes sparkled, her genuine smile a mirror of the chauffeur's. "Victor, it's wonderful to see you again."

"The pleasure is all mine, Lady Hawthorne," he responded, with a respectful bow.

Beside them, Aunt Beatrice observed the exchange, her posture regal, her expression guarded. A slight incline of her head acknowledged Victor's presence.

Sensing the older woman's reserve, Victor turned his attention back to the task at hand.

With a fluid motion, he opened the motorcar door, the polished handle gleaming in the afternoon light. "Shall we proceed to the hotel?"

Meli leaned closer to Elizabeth, a mischievous twinkle in her eye, her voice a hushed, excited murmur. "His accent is so ... French." She mimicked the chauffeur's intonation playfully, her smile broadening.

Elizabeth chuckled, shaking her head in amusement. "What were you expecting in Cannes, Dutch?" she teased, her gaze following the chauffeur as he moved with poised efficiency. The light banter eased the weariness of travel, drawing a shared moment of laughter that brightened their arrival.

Aunt Beatrice tutted, casting a disapproving look over her shoulder at the cousins.

Elizabeth caught Meli's eye, a fleeting glint of amusement shared between them before their expressions smoothed into the appropriate decorum under Aunt Beatrice's watchful eye.

Elizabeth turned to Aunt Beatrice, extending her arm for support. "Shall we, Aunt?"

Aunt Beatrice's lips tightened momentarily, revealing her hesitation, yet she linked her arm with Elizabeth's. They stepped into the waiting Rolls-Royce, settling into the burgundy leather seats that emitted a soft sigh under their weight. The dashboard's polished walnut gleamed, bathed in the waning sunlight streaming through the windows.

As Victor engaged the engine, the motorcar purred to life with a low, rhythmic vibration that thrummed through the cabin. They pulled away from the Cannes train station, where the clamour of arriving and departing trains mixed with the chatter of well-heeled travellers and the occasional shrill of a whistle. Meli pressed her face against the window, her eyes widening with wonder as the cityscape unfolded before them.

They soon entered a section of the city where the architecture began to transform. The roads, lined with young plane trees just shedding their last leaves, framed views of art nouveau façades interspersed with the more subdued Belle époque styles that marked the city's affluence. Each elegant building seemed to captivate Meli, drawing her gaze as they whizzed past.

The drive took them along a route flush with small boutiques and cafés whose tables spilled onto the sidewalks, patrons languishing over espresso and pastries under elegant awnings. Meli's reflection in the window mirrored the lively street scenes, her expression a mixture of delight and curiosity. Occasionally, she would point out glimpses of the sea peeking through alleyways, the azure teases promising the proximity of the Mediterranean.

Victor navigated with ease, his familiarity with the route evident as he manoeuvred around a slow-moving delivery cart laden with crates of local citrus and flowers destined for one of the grand hotels. Meli's enthusiasm didn't wane; she soaked in every detail.

Soon, they reached the renowned Boulevard de la Croisette, and Elizabeth leaned forward, captivated by the dazzling panorama unfolding before them. Ahead, the Mediterranean stretched out like an endless expanse of azure silk, its undulating waves lapping against the wide, sand-swept shoreline. A bracing, salt-tinged breeze swept across the promenade, rustling the dense fronds of the towering palm trees that lined the boulevard like the pages of a well-worn novel.

Ornate hotels and high-end boutiques flanked the bustling thoroughfare, their façades a marvel of intricate stonework, ornamental balconies, and gleaming windows.

Splashes of colour drew the eye as the fashionable set paraded along the promenade. Ladies in striking beaded dresses and smart fur-trimmed coats strolled arm in arm with gentlemen in dapper suits and jaunty fedoras. Laughter and lively chatter filled the air, underscoring the *joie de vivre* that France was so famous for.

Beside Elizabeth, Meli's attention was captured by the vibrant life swirling around them on the Boulevard. Her excitement peaked as a gleaming Hispano-Suiza motorcar coasted past, its polished contours gleaming in the sun's fading rays. The driver, a handsome young man with tousled dark hair and an engaging smile, tipped his hat in a playful, gallant gesture, sparking a delighted grin on Meli's face. Meli's laughter, light and free, filled the air, drawing a stern look from Aunt Beatrice, whose displeasure was as pronounced as a cold draught in a warm parlour.

Elizabeth's gaze lingered on Meli, her brow furrowing. She adored her young cousin, yet Meli's impulsive decisions often courted danger. One whim – to explore beyond her Greek homeland – had led Meli to stow away aboard the SS Andromeda. That act of curiosity plunged her into a dire ordeal, entangling her in a murder investigation that threatened her life. As Meli's carefree demeanour caught Elizabeth's eye, memories constricted her chest. Meli's vibrant spirit both charmed and worried her, a constant source of concern.

The Rolls-Royce veered off the lively Boulevard de la Croisette, coming to a stop in front of Le Majestique Palais de Cannes. The grand limestone façade of the hotel loomed impressively as the doormen, clad in sharp maroon and gold livery, descended on the motorcar. They handled the luggage with efficient precision, while Elizabeth, Aunt Beatrice, Meli, and Evelyn alighted onto the cobblestone driveway.

As always, Elizabeth's gaze gravitated towards the imposing Le Majestique Palais de Cannes. No matter how often she visited, its beauty always captivated her. The cream-coloured limestone bathed in the pale winter sun exuded a quiet opulence. Above, the balconies displayed a network of scrollwork so intricate it seemed as if spun from iron lace.

At the heart of the frontage, ornate columns flanked the grand arched entryway, lending a regal air to the approach. Overhead, a striking iron canopy, detailed with fine filigree, marked the entrance, setting it apart from the smooth stone backdrop. The hotel's name, displayed in the elegant gold script above the arch, glinted in the fading winter sun.

Windows, tall and commanding, lined the façade, their glass catching the light and throwing back splashes of the azure sky and verdant palm fronds that swayed lazily in the breeze. The stone around each window was carved with the precision of an artist's hand, floral patterns swirling into geometric designs that drew the eye ever upward to the ornate cornice crowning the building.

Beside her, Meli's eyes widened in awe at the grand façade. She leaned closer to Elizabeth, her voice a hushed murmur filled with excitement. "Oh, Elizabeth, it's positively breathtaking!"

A tall, meticulously groomed man strode forward, his bearing exuding refined sophistication. His eyes, sharp and appraising, swept over the group before settling on Aunt Beatrice. "Lady Hawthorne, welcome back to Le Majestique Palais de Cannes," he announced, his voice smooth and cultured, the lilting cadence of the Riviera pronounced in his speech. "I am Henri Marchand, the new manager. It is a pleasure to make your acquaintance."

Aunt Beatrice surveyed the grand entrance with an air of unmistakable displeasure. "I was expecting Monsieur Gáston to be here to greet us," she pronounced, her tone clipped and laced with thinly veiled irritation. "He's always been such an attentive host at the Majestique.

Sensing her aunt's discomfort, Elizabeth placed a comforting hand on her aunt's arm, offering a placating smile. "I'm certain Monsieur Marchand will prove just as attentive, Aunt."

"Of course," Monsieur Marchand assured her. "Lady Hawthorne, my staff and I are at your disposal."

Aunt Beatrice's expression remained guarded as she inclined her head in the barest of acknowledgments.

Undeterred, Monsieur Marchand turned his attention to Elizabeth, his lips curving into a warm smile. "Please, allow me to escort you inside."

He led them through the grand arched entryway into the opulent foyer. Aunt Beatrice's shoulders tensed slightly, the change in management clearly weighing on her mind.

Inside, Meli's eyes widened in awe at the soaring ceiling, gleaming marble floors, and the ornate furnishings that adorned the space. "Elizabeth, it's like stepping into another world," she whispered, her voice filled with wonder.

Elizabeth reached out and gave Meli's hand a gentle squeeze, reminding her cousin to maintain her composure under Aunt Beatrice's critical gaze.

Elizabeth observed Aunt Beatrice, noting the unmistakable traces of past sorrows in her aunt's bearing. The heavy velvets she favoured mirrored her emotional state, serving as both marks of status and shields against change. These gowns, like the walls around her heart, protected her from the tides that had swept away her dearest loves. Tragedy had sculpted Aunt Beatrice's worldview: first Teddy, her only child, lost before her fifth birthday, then Arthur, her beloved husband.

The presence of a new manager was, in the grand scheme of things, a minor event. Yet to Aunt Beatrice, it represented another small erosion of the world she knew, a world where Teddy's laughter and Arthur's steady presence still echoed in the corners of her memory. Elizabeth understood that her aunt's resistance to change was not merely a preference but a necessity, an effort to maintain a connection to a past that felt less fractured than the present.

Chapter Two

SUNLIGHT FILTERED THROUGH THE sheer curtains of Elizabeth's room at Le Majestique, rousing her from a peaceful slumber. The faint rustle of silk against cotton from the other side of the room hinted at Meli's restlessness.

She stretched languidly, relishing the softness of the Egyptian cotton sheets against her skin. The distant murmur of the sea mingled with the cheerful chatter of birds outside her window, a melodious reminder that she was far from the familiar sounds of London.

Elizabeth eased out of bed, the morning air brushing against her skin. She tied her silk robe securely at the waist, the smooth fabric sliding into a neat knot. She crossed the room, her bare feet sinking into the plush carpet with each step.

With a gentle push, she opened the French doors, welcoming the pleasant February morning air. The salty scent of the Mediterranean mixed with the delicate fragrance of blooming flowers from the gardens below. The Boulevard de la Croisette was stirring to life – shopkeepers arranging their displays, early risers strolling along the promenade.

Elizabeth leaned against the iron railing, her hazel eyes taking in the vibrant scene. Below, the grand hotels and fashionable boutiques lining the boulevard stood gleaming in the early morning light. The Riviera was waking, its pulse quickening with the rising sun.

Behind her, the rustle of sheets and a soft yawn signalled Meli's awakening. Elizabeth turned, smiling at the sight of her cousin stretching amid the rumpled linens of her twin bed.

"Good morning, Meli," Elizabeth called, her smile softening as she watched her cousin stretch among the rumpled sheets.

Meli blinked, her toffee-coloured eyes struggling to focus. "Elizabeth, you're up early," she mumbled, dark curls framing her face as she sat up. "Though I can see why – it looks as if it's going to be a beautiful day."

"I wanted to take in the sights and sounds of Cannes before the city shakes off its slumber," Elizabeth replied, gesturing to the bustling boulevard.

Meli leapt out of bed, her robe billowing behind her as she rushed to Elizabeth's side. Gripping the ornate railing, she leaned forward, her toffee-coloured eyes widening with delight as they drank in the vibrant scene below. "Oh, Elizabeth, it's even more beautiful than I imagined." Her voice was breathless with excitement. "The people, the shops, the cafés – I want to explore every inch."

A warm smile tugged at Elizabeth's lips as she watched her cousin's unbridled enthusiasm. She placed a gentle hand on Meli's arm, feeling the younger woman's energy thrumming beneath her touch. "There's no need to rush. We have all day to discover the delights of Cannes."

Meli whirled to face Elizabeth, her eyes sparkling. "I know, I know. But can you blame me for being excited?" She pirouetted, her robe flaring out like a dancer's skirt.

Elizabeth's lips quirked into a smile. "Aunt Beatrice might, if we dash out before hearing her plans." She arched an eyebrow. "And I'd rather not explain why you swooned from hunger in the middle of the Boulevard de la Croisette. Perhaps we should fortify ourselves with some breakfast first?"

Laughter bubbled up from Meli, light and effervescent. "Oh, all right. Breakfast first, then adventure!" She linked her arm through Elizabeth's, eyes sparkling.

Elizabeth's smile softened. "We must be mindful of Aunt Beatrice, Meli. She'd never admit it, but she's not as spry as she once was."

"You're right," Meli nodded, then leaned in with a mischievous grin. "Though I'm sure she'll always have the energy to find you a husband."

Elizabeth rolled her eyes, turning to gaze at the bustling Cannes below. "I think Aunt Beatrice understands that, even if she gets carried away with her matchmaking." Elizabeth's voice softened. "Love is the only match I'll accept, Meli. Nothing less."

With a gentle tug on Meli's arm, Elizabeth steered them towards the bedroom. "Now, let's get dressed. We'll see if Aunt Beatrice and Evelyn are ready for breakfast."

Meli nodded, her expression shifting to one of excitement once more. She darted past Elizabeth, diving into the shared wardrobe with an enthusiasm that made the hangers rattle.

Elizabeth shook her head, a fond smile playing on her lips at Meli's fervour. She moved to her own side of the wardrobe, her fingers skimming over the array of fabrics until they settled on a day dress.

Elizabeth donned a dress in a soft shade of green, reminiscent of spring's first leaves. Light cotton fabric suited the mild Cannes weather. The fitted bodice featured a modest scoop neckline and short, puffed sleeves. From the waist, the skirt's soft pleats fell to just above her ankles, creating an elegant silhouette.

Her fingers deftly fastened the delicate pearl buttons running down the bodice. She smoothed her dark bob, the sleek strands framing her face. With a light touch, she dabbed rouge onto her cheeks and swept rose pink lipstick across her lips.

Elizabeth gave her reflection a final appraising glance. Satisfied, she turned from the mirror, ready to begin the day.

Elizabeth entered the sitting room. Aunt Beatrice and Evelyn looked up as she approached.

"Good morning, Aunt Beatrice, Evelyn," Elizabeth greeted them warmly.

Aunt Beatrice's sapphire eyes met Elizabeth's, a mixture of fondness and mild reproach in her gaze. "Ah, Elizabeth. I was beginning to wonder if you and Meli had taken root in your beds."

"Not at all, Aunt. Meli's practically vibrating with excitement to explore Cannes."

As if on cue, Meli bounded into the room, her floral dress swishing around her knees. "Good morning, everyone! Isn't it just the most perfect day?"

Aunt Beatrice raised an eyebrow, her tone stern but her eyes twinkling. "Indeed, Meli. Now, shall we proceed?"

Elizabeth and Meli gathered their belongings, exchanging a quick glance as Aunt Beatrice and Evelyn headed for the grand staircase. Aunt Beatrice's disdain for modern conveniences was as predictable as the tide.

"We'll meet you in the lobby," Elizabeth called out, steering Meli towards the lift.

The attendant greeted them with a crisp nod as they stepped into the brass-trimmed cabin. As the doors slid shut, Meli leaned in, her voice barely above a whisper.

"How long do you think it'll take Aunt Beatrice to notice we've beaten her down?" Meli asked.

Elizabeth raised an eyebrow as the lift descended, depositing them in the marble-clad foyer long before the clip of Aunt Beatrice's heels were heard on the stairs.

The grand reception area buzzed with activity as Elizabeth and Meli waited for Aunt Beatrice and Evelyn. A shrill voice cut through the ambient chatter, drawing Elizabeth's attention to the reception desk.

"Monsieur Marchand, my emerald necklace is gone!" An elegantly dressed older woman stood before the hotel manager, her voice quivering. Her knuckles whitened as she gripped her purse. "I am certain I left it in my room safe and it's not there anymore. You must call the police."

Henri Marchand's composed expression never faltered. He placed his hand on the woman's arm, his voice low and steady. "Madame Dupont, please try to stay calm. I believe you placed your necklace in the main safe." He caught the eye of a nearby receptionist. "As soon as Armand, our head of security, arrives, I will retrieve it for you."

Madame Dupont's hands trembled, her brow creased with worry. "But I was so sure ... I remember placing it in the safe in my room last night." Uncertainty clouded her features as her voice trailed off.

Monsieur Marchand nodded, his gaze sympathetic. "Our mind often plays tricks on us. It's easily done." With a discreet motion, he summoned a receptionist. "Please escort Madame Dupont back to her room."

Elizabeth and Meli watched the scene unfold, their eyes wide. As the receptionist guided Madame Dupont towards the lift, Elizabeth leaned in, whispering, "That poor woman. I can't imagine how distressing it must be to lose something so valuable."

"Are we talking about her mind or her jewellery?" Meli asked.

Elizabeth considered for a moment. "A sharp mind is the most valuable accessory a woman can possess. It never goes out of style and only grows more valuable with time."

As Madame Dupont's uncertain steps faded, Monsieur Marchand approached Elizabeth. He leaned in, his voice low. "Madame Dupont's memory has been ... unreliable of late. This is the third time she's misplaced her jewels this week."

Elizabeth's brow furrowed. "How distressing for her."

"Indeed. We do what we can, but..." Marchand's shoulders rose and fell. "Time marches on for us all."

"Some faster than others, it seems," Elizabeth murmured.

Marchand nodded. "If you'll excuse me, Lady Elizabeth." He turned, striding back to the reception desk.

Elizabeth watched him go, her mind pondering poor Madame Dupont's misfortune.

Elizabeth scanned the lobby, her gaze landing on Aunt Beatrice. The older woman approached, flanked by Evelyn and an unfamiliar gentleman. Elizabeth nudged Meli, and they exchanged a curious glance.

"Elizabeth, Meli," Aunt Beatrice said, "This is Mr Thomas Gray."

The man stepped forward. "A pleasure, ladies," he drawled, his accent distinctly Southern.

Elizabeth studied Mr Gray. His salt-and-pepper hair complemented a clean-shaven, rugged face. His tailored suit emphasised broad shoulders and a commanding presence.

Mr Gray lifted Meli's hand to his lips. "Enchanted, mademoiselle."

Meli giggled, clearly charmed. Even Aunt Beatrice seemed unusually animated in his company.

Elizabeth, however, held back. Despite Mr Gray's undeniable charisma, something about him gave her pause. His blue eyes, while warm, held a hint of calculation.

As introductions continued, Elizabeth wondered about the true nature of Mr Thomas Gray.

"Mr Gray was kind enough to assist me when I almost lost my footing on the stairs," Aunt Beatrice explained, her gaze darting to Evelyn. A flicker of annoyance passed over her features, so fleeting that Elizabeth almost missed it. "Evelyn had forgotten something in our suite and had returned to collect it. I'm afraid I grew impatient and went on without her, and that's when Mr Gray's prompt action prevented a rather unpleasant tumble."

Mr Gray waved off the praise, his hand cutting a lazy arc through the air. "Hardly worth mentioning, I assure you." The words rolled off his tongue, smooth as honey, betraying his Charleston roots.

"As much as I would love to continue this delightful conversation, I'm afraid I have a prior engagement that I must attend to," Mr Gray said, a hint of regret lacing his words. "But I hope our paths will cross again soon." His gaze lingered on Elizabeth for a moment before he turned to address the group. "It has been an absolute pleasure making your acquaintance."

Mr Gray offered a warm smile and a graceful bow before taking his leave.

As he departed, Elizabeth noticed Meli's gaze lingering on his retreating figure. She pondered her own conflicting impressions of their new acquaintance - his effortless charm at odds with the shrewd look she'd caught in his eyes.

"Shall we proceed to breakfast?" Aunt Beatrice asked, already turning towards the hotel's dining area.

They entered Le Jardin Matin, where sunlight streamed through tall windows framing the Croisette. The room hummed with quiet conversation and the clink of silverware. Waiters glided between tables, balancing trays of steaming coffee and fresh pastries.

As they settled near a window, Elizabeth caught the eye of an approaching waiter. "Perhaps a selection for the table?" she suggested. "Croissants, fresh fruit, pastries, and tea?"

Aunt Beatrice nodded her approval.

"Certainly, Lady Hawthorne," the waiter said, departing with a slight bow.

"I can't wait to explore," Meli said, her eyes sparkling. "There's so much to see!"

Elizabeth glanced at Aunt Beatrice, anticipating a clash between youthful enthusiasm and traditional expectations. But her aunt's attention was elsewhere, fixed on a group across the room.

"Isn't that Alexander Cavendish?"

Aunt Beatrice's brow furrowed slightly, her lips pursed.

"Alexander?" Elizabeth pressed, curious about her aunt's reaction. "Are you certain, Aunt?"

Aunt Beatrice nodded, her gaze fixed on Alexander's table. "Yes, that's him. I'm positive."

"Who are those women?" Elizabeth asked, noting her aunt's tense posture.

"I don't recognise them," Aunt Beatrice replied, her voice tight. "But he seems rather ... familiar with their company."

Meli, looking up from her croissant, followed their gaze. "Who's Alexander?"

"Alexander Cavendish, the Earl of Wexford, with a grand estate in the south of England," Aunt Beatrice explained, her tone softening.

"His mother and I were first cousins, more like sisters."

"Is one of those women his wife?" Meli asked, craning her neck for a better view.

Aunt Beatrice shook her head, a rueful smile playing on her lips. "No, Alexander has never married, despite my best efforts." She sighed, her gaze drifting back to the Earl's table. "His late father, God rest his soul, had a rather unfortunate gambling habit that left the estate in a very precarious financial state, which limits his options. I can't imagine what brings him to Cannes, though."

Elizabeth felt a twinge of sympathy for Alexander, understanding the weight of family expectations.

"We should make our presence known," Aunt Beatrice declared, that familiar determined gleam in her eye. She rose. "Come, Elizabeth."

As Evelyn made to stand, Aunt Beatrice waved her back. "Finish your breakfast, Evelyn. We shan't be long."

Elizabeth followed her aunt across the room, her heart quickening as they neared Alexander's table. The Earl's head snapped up, his eyes widening and the colour draining from his face.

"Aunt Beatrice! Elizabeth!" Alexander sprang to his feet.

Aunt Beatrice's eyes crinkled with affection. "Alexander, my dear boy. What a pleasant surprise to find you here in Cannes." Her gaze flicked to the two women accompanying him, narrowing as she assessed their pedigree and social standing.

Alexander's hand swept in an elegant arc, a nervous edge to his movements. "Aunt Beatrice, Elizabeth, allow me to introduce Mrs Laura Hicks and her daughter, Miss Clara Hicks."

Elizabeth noted how Alexander's expression softened when introducing the younger woman. A delicate blush coloured Miss Hicks's cheeks under his gaze. Clara's auburn hair framed her face in soft waves, her dark eyes warm and inviting as she glanced at Alexander with a touch of shyness.

"Ladies, this is my aunt, the dowager Lady Hawthorne, and Lady Elizabeth Hawthorne."

Aunt Beatrice leaned forward, her tone carrying a hint of expectation. "Hicks, did you say? Any relation to the Pendlebury-Hicks?"

"I don't think so." Mrs Hicks's reply carried a faint trace of a Pennsylvanian accent, the vowels rounded distinctively.

Disappointment flickered across Aunt Beatrice's features. "Oh, you're American."

Mrs Hicks's chin lifted slightly, a subtle challenge in her posture. "Pittsburgh born and raised."

Aunt Beatrice's lips thinned, her tone clipped. "Indeed."

Elizabeth stepped forward, her warm smile and extended hand a gesture of welcome. "Pleased to meet you Mrs Hicks, Miss Hicks. Although I've never visited that particular region, I understand Pennsylvania boasts some of the most breathtaking scenery, particularly the Alleghenies."

Mrs Hicks's perfectly shaped brow arched, her response pointed. "I'm impressed, Lady Elizabeth. Most people outside of America think Pennsylvania consists only of steel mills and coal mines."

Aunt Beatrice turned to Alexander, pointedly ignoring Mrs Hicks's barb. "And how long will you be staying in Cannes, Alexander?"

Alexander's gaze darted to Miss Hicks, a hint of uncertainty in his voice. "I'm not sure."

Aunt Beatrice's brow furrowed, her lips pursing into a moue of disapproval as her gaze swept appraisingly over Clara. "I see. Well, in that case, I must insist you join the family for dinner this evening." She placed a possessive hand on Alexander's arm, her grip firm. "I'm sure Mrs Hicks and her daughter can spare you this evening."

Mrs Hicks maintained her saccharine smile, though a glint of challenge sparked in her eyes. "Of course, Lady Hawthorne. We wouldn't dream of keeping Alexander from you this evening." She emphasised Aunt Beatrice's title, a hint of condescension in her tone. "And Alexander is a grown man, free to do as he pleases."

The use of Alexander's first name, rather than the more formal Lord Cavendish, was a deliberate slight, meant to irk the prim dowager. Mrs Hicks subtly angled her body to shield Clara from Aunt Beatrice's scrutiny, a protective instinct betrayed only by the tightening of her jaw.

Aunt Beatrice's nostrils flared slightly at Mrs Hicks's casual dismissal, but she recovered quickly, her smile becoming strained at the edges.

Elizabeth's heart went out to Alexander as she watched Aunt Beatrice's forceful personality envelop him. She knew her aunt's intentions were bourne out of concern, even if her manner could seem overbearing at times. Still, she could see the strain creeping across Alexander's features.

Alexander's shoulders sagged slightly, resignation in his voice. "Of course, Aunt, I'd be delighted."

Aunt Beatrice flashed a look of triumph at Mrs Hicks before resting on her nephew. "Very well. Alexander, I shall expect you at seven o'clock sharp. Don't be late."

She spun on her heel, her satisfied smile tugging at her lips as she led the way.

Elizabeth watched her aunt, noting the satisfaction in her stride. She glanced at Alexander, observing the resignation in his posture and the lingering gaze he cast towards Miss Hicks. It was clear he had a soft spot for her. Reflecting on Aunt Beatrice's relentless quest to find the Earl a suitable wife, Elizabeth realised an American was not part of her aunt's vision for the future Duchess. The evening ahead promised to be a delicate dance of intentions and ambitions, with Aunt Beatrice leading the charge.

Chapter Three

ELIZABETH SAT BEFORE THE triptych mirror on the vanity, her brush gliding through her hair. The glossy inky strands fell in a sleek, straight curtain around her expertly made-up face. She studied her reflection and smiled, content after a day filled with simple pleasures and familial companionship.

Fastening her mother's pearls around her neck, Elizabeth's thoughts wandered to the day's adventures. Strolling along the Boulevard de la Croisette with Meli, Aunt Beatrice, and Evelyn had been delightful. The vibrant sights and sounds of the promenade – the sparkling Mediterranean, the warm sun, the parade of fashionable people – had created a truly captivating experience.

Meli's excitement had been infectious, her toffee-coloured eyes sparkling as she pointed out every fashionable woman they encountered. "Look, Elizabeth, did you see that woman's hat? And her dress – so elegant!" Her cousin's enthusiasm had been a joy to witness.

In contrast, Aunt Beatrice had shared her observations with a hint of melancholy. "So many new shops and such a lively atmosphere. It's not quite the Cannes I remember." Elizabeth had noted the wistful expression that flickered across her aunt's features, her gaze lingering on the bustling promenade.

Meli's voice pulled Elizabeth from her reverie. "Elizabeth, do you think Aunt Beatrice will let us visit the casino later?" Meli emerged from the ensuite, eyes wide with anticipation, her fingers twisting a strand of her dark curls.

Elizabeth turned, smiling. "You know Aunt Beatrice doesn't approve of gambling, Meli."

Meli sighed, frustration edging her voice. "I know, but I've never been to a casino before. I imagine it's very glamorous."

Elizabeth offered a conciliatory smile. "We have the opera to look forward to tomorrow evening. I'm sure that will be a night to remember." She reached out, giving her cousin's hand a reassuring squeeze.

Meli nodded, though the sparkle in her eyes dimmed slightly. Elizabeth rose from the vanity, smoothing the delicate chiffon of her dress with care. "Now, let's hurry. We don't want to keep Aunt Beatrice waiting."

After a final glance in the mirror, Meli and Elizabeth hurried to the sitting room, where Aunt Beatrice and Evelyn waited. Aunt Beatrice sat upright, her posture rigid. She glanced up from her gold watch, eyes narrowing slightly as they entered.

"Do hurry, girls." She tapped her watch with a jewelled finger and sighed, eyes lifting heavenward. "Punctuality is a virtue, one that you young ones seem all too ready to overlook."

Elizabeth clasped her hands together. "I'm sorry, Aunt Beatrice. The fault is mine; I couldn't decide which earrings to wear, and time got away from me." She offered an apologetic smile.

Aunt Beatrice's lips twitched as she suppressed a smile. She rose, the emerald silk of her gown whispering against the chair. "Indeed, but we mustn't let fashion make us forget our manners."

Elizabeth stepped forward and held the door open, gesturing for Aunt Beatrice and Evelyn to step into the hallway. "Shall we, Aunt?"

Meli paused in front of the lift. "Aunt Beatrice, wouldn't you like to try the lift, just this once? It's much quicker and perfectly safe."

Aunt Beatrice tightened her grip on her purse and cast a wary glance at the lift. "My dear, I have no intention of entrusting my well-being to a contraption suspended in mid-air by a mere thread. Stairs have served us well enough for centuries, and I prefer the reliability of my two feet, thank you very much."

Noticing Evelyn's eager look toward the lift, Meli seized the moment. "Evelyn, you'll join me, won't you?"

Evelyn hesitated, glancing at Aunt Beatrice. The older woman gave a slight nod. "Go ahead, Evelyn. Though this fascination with speed and convenience is quite beyond me," she added with a small huff.

Elizabeth linked her arm with her aunt's. "Then we'll take the scenic route. The exercise will do us good, and it's the perfect opportunity to admire the hotel's architecture a bit more closely."

Meli grinned as Evelyn stepped toward her. "It's settled then! We'll see who reaches the bottom first!" she chirped, waving as the lift doors closed.

Aunt Beatrice watched them go, then began her steady descent with Elizabeth. "Everything's such a whirlwind these days," she muttered, gripping the railing firmly. "The old ways had order. Everyone knew their place and what was expected of them."

Elizabeth linked her arm with her aunt's. "That's true, Aunt. But sometimes, change can bring new opportunities." She guided them down the staircase, wondering if they were no longer just talking about the lift, but perhaps Alexander and his apparent attachment to Miss Hicks.

They descended the last steps of the grand staircase into the foyer, where Meli and Evelyn awaited. Meli's face brightened with a triumphant smile, pleased at having won their playful race.

"Ah, there you are." Meli bounced on her toes. "We were beginning to think a search party might be needed to rescue you from those endless stairs."

Aunt Beatrice arched an eyebrow, her gaze lingering on Meli. "Patience, my dear Meli, is a virtue you'd do well to cultivate."

Meli's smile softened, though her eyes still danced with mischief. "I shall endeavour to remember that, Aunt Beatrice." She exchanged a quick, amused glance with Elizabeth.

Elizabeth scanned the dining room as they entered, her gaze settling on Alexander. He sat at the table, rising to greet them with a warm smile that didn't quite reach his eyes. A hint of tension lingered in the set of his shoulders.

"I trust you've all had a pleasant day?" Alexander's gaze swept across the group, lingering on Elizabeth.

Aunt Beatrice's sharp eyes scanned the bustling room as they took their seats. She signalled a waiter. "It's rather busy tonight. Is there something special happening?"

The waiter nodded. "Indeed, Lady Hawthorne. Many of our guests are here for the art auction taking place in a few days. It's quite the event."

"An art auction, you say?" Aunt Beatrice raised an eyebrow. "I wasn't aware of that." She turned her gaze to Alexander. "Did you know about this?"

Alexander adjusted his cuffs, his gaze flicking away. "No, first I'm hearing of it." His voice carried a tight edge. Elizabeth sensed his unease and felt a twinge of concern.

Aunt Beatrice's eyes lit up with interest. "Perhaps we should attend."

Alexander's fingers tapped a soft rhythm on the tablecloth. "I, uh, you know what these things are like. All the decent pieces will have been reserved in advance. Besides, you have a rather splendid collection at Hawthorne Hall, Aunt."

Elizabeth noticed his jaw tightening. "And," he continued, more slowly, "these auctions can be rather long and tiresome. And with so many people, it might be difficult to find good seats."

"Perhaps we might consider Christie's in London, Aunt." Elizabeth turned to her aunt.

Aunt Beatrice pursed her lips, considering. "Very well. But I do hope we won't miss out on something exceptional."

Alexander exhaled, his shoulders easing a fraction. Yet Elizabeth could still see shadows of worry in his eyes.

As they perused the menu, Elizabeth's gaze flicked to Alexander. His fingers tapped the tablecloth, pausing only when Aunt Beatrice glanced his way."Have you given any more thought to the matter we've been discussing in our correspondence?"

Alexander's fork clinked against his plate. "I'm working on it, Aunt Beatrice."

Aunt Beatrice set down her wineglass. "It sounds to me like you're avoiding the issue."

Alexander straightened in his chair, his jaw tensing. "I assure you, I am taking steps."

Aunt Beatrice sighed, her eyes softening, yet the determination in her voice remained firm. "Alexander, it is your duty to ensure the continuation of the Wexford line, not to mention maintaining the estate. The mismanagement and debts left by your father's gambling habit have put everything at risk."

Alexander's grip on his fork tightened, his face flushing. "I am well aware of my responsibilities." His voice was strained but controlled.

Aunt Beatrice leaned forward, her voice lowering but maintaining its firmness. "If you can't find a suitable wife soon, I will have to take matters into my own hands. I owe it to your mother – my dear cousin, who was like a sister to me – to see that our family's legacy is preserved."

Alexander glanced down at his plate, then back at his aunt, frustration and resignation flickering in his eyes. "As I said, Aunt, the matter is in hand."

Aunt Beatrice reached out, placing a hand over his in a rare gesture of tenderness. "I know it isn't easy, but this is the path we must walk. Our rank comes with responsibilities. It's what generations of our ancestors have always done – put duty before personal feelings."

Alexander nodded stiffly, his face a mask of composure, but Elizabeth could see the storm brewing beneath. His shoulders were rigid. Elizabeth felt a pang of sympathy, her own heart aching at the sight of her cousin's struggle, ensnared in a web of duty and obligation. She offered him a small, supportive smile, hoping to convey her understanding and solidarity.

In many ways, Alexander's situation was no different to her own – both were expected to marry purely to satisfy societal expectations, regardless of their own wants. Elizabeth couldn't help but wonder if he, too, had dreams and aspirations that lay beyond the confines of duty and propriety.

As Aunt Beatrice launched into a detailed list of potential suitors she had in mind for Alexander, Elizabeth's gaze drifted to her cousin's face. Though he maintained an attentive façade, she caught the fleeting flicker of his eyes, drawn towards where Miss Clara Hicks sat across the room. Elizabeth's heart went out to him; she knew all too well the silent yearning for freedom to live one's own life, unencumbered by the demands of family and society.

Aunt Beatrice's voice droned on, oblivious to the subtle turmoil playing out before her. Elizabeth pressed her lips together, feeling a pang of sympathy for Alexander, even as she wondered if another had already claimed his heart.

Elizabeth's attention snapped to the striking figure entering the dining room. Clad in a flowing gown of deep plum that accentuated her figure and flared at the hem, she glided towards their table. Her confident stride commanded the room, her smile warm, her lingering gaze on Alexander hinting at a shared history.

"Lord Cavendish." She leaned in, her movements smooth and deliberate, her hand brushing his arm. "We missed you at tennis today." The princess's words carried the crisp, refined tones of one raised by an English nanny.

Alexander's cheeks flushed. He fidgeted with his cufflinks. "I, er … had some urgent business to attend to."

A delicate brow arched as she tsked, a mischievous glint in her eye. "That's a shame. I was so looking forward to our match."

Elizabeth watched, her amusement barely concealed. The colour in her cousin's cheeks deepened as the table's attention fixed on him.

"Aren't you going to introduce me?" She tilted her head, fingers brushing the diamond choker at her neck.

Alexander cleared his throat, his gaze darting nervously. He gestured towards Aunt Beatrice. "This is my aunt, the dowager Lady Hawthorne."

Beatrice inclined her head, her discerning gaze sweeping over the newcomer.

"My cousin, Lady Elizabeth," Alexander said. He nodded to each in turn. "Miss Melina Diomaros and my aunt's companion, Miss Evelyn Brown."

He paused, a flicker of hesitation crossing his face. "May I present Princess Sofia de' Medici."

Aunt Beatrice straightened in her chair. Her gaze swept over the princess before settling on her face. "Your Highness, a pleasure to make your acquaintance."

Aunt Beatrice's gaze swept the room. "And is your husband with you this evening, Your Highness?"

Princess Sofia's smile faltered. "I'm not married. My dinner companion cancelled, so I'm dining alone tonight."

Elizabeth caught the quick upturn of her aunt's lips, a gleam flickering in her eyes.

Aunt Beatrice's hand swept towards the empty chair. "Well, that simply won't do. Please, join us."

Alexander's gaze flicked between the two women, worry forming a faint crease between his brows. He cleared his throat, a note of unease in his voice. "Aunt, I'm sure the princess has other plans. We wouldn't want to impose."

Sofia's gaze lingered on Alexander, a coy smile playing on her crimson lips. "I would be delighted," she purred, settling into the chair beside him. "And please, I hate all that stuffy nonsense. Call me Sofia."

Aunt Beatrice leaned forward, her eyes narrowing with curiosity. "What brings you to Cannes, Your Highn ... Sofia?"

Sofia's smile faded as she answered. "With so many of my friends now married, I find myself with rather too much time on my hands. So I've been indulging in an extended tour of the Riviera." Her eyes flicked toward Alexander, a hint of mischief dancing in their depths. "That's how

I first met Alexander – we were both staying at the same hotel in St Tropez."

Alexander shifted uncomfortably, the muscle in his jaw tightening. Elizabeth could see Aunt Beatrice's gaze darting between him and Sofia, no doubt cataloguing the princess as a potential match for the Wexford title.

A distant sadness flickered across Beatrice's face as she spoke. "I understand only too well what loneliness is." She let out a soft sigh, her shoulders slumping. "But I'm sure there is no shortage of eligible men vying for your affections."

Sofia's smile held a rueful edge. "Indeed there are, but none of them are what you would call the marrying type." Her eyes drifted towards Alexander, a warmth kindling within their depths as she regarded him.

Alexander's fingers tightened around the base of his wineglass as his gaze darted towards Miss Hicks's table. He brought the glass to his lips, draining half the contents in one defiant gulp, then set it down on the table with a dull thud that drew a sharp, disapproving glance from Aunt Beatrice.

"And what of your family?" Aunt Beatrice continued, returning her attention to the princess. "Do you have any siblings?"

Sofia's expression clouded. "Unfortunately, not. I am all alone in the world since my parents passed away." A note of sorrow edged her words.

"How sad." Aunt Beatrice's brow creased with a hint of compassion. "For there is no greater treasure than one's family."

A discreet cough cut through their conversation, drawing all eyes to the edge of the table where Monsieur Marchand hovered.

"Pardon the interruption, Your Highness," he said, his voice low and urgent. "But there is a most pressing telephone call for you in the reception area."

Sofia's brow pinched. "Please inform them I am otherwise engaged at present, and whatever it is can wait until morning." She waved a dismissive hand.

Elizabeth couldn't help but notice the almost imperceptible tightening of his jaw as he persisted. "I'm afraid the caller was most insistent, Your Highness."

She watched the exchange. Marchand's determined manner struck a discordant note, leaving her to wonder what could be so pressing as to warrant such a breach of protocol by Monsieur Marchand.

With a sigh, Sofia got to her feet. "Very well, if I must." The princess offered an apologetic nod before following Monsieur Marchand out of the dining room.

Aunt Beatrice tsked disapprovingly once the princess had departed. "Monsieur Marchand's behaviour was most impertinent. I've a good mind to speak to him about it. Monsieur Gáston would never have spoken to someone of Princess Sofia's rank in such a way."

Elizabeth nodded, her brow furrowed in thought. "Indeed, it was a most curious breach of etiquette." Slipping one of her gloves inside her purse, Elizabeth rose from her seat. "If you'll excuse me, I believe I've misplaced one of my gloves."

Elizabeth slipped out of the dining room, making her way towards the hotel reception. As she approached a discreet alcove, raised voices drew her attention. Peering around the corner, she found Princess Sofia and Monsieur Marchand locked in a heated exchange.

The princess stood rigid, her gestures sharp and agitated as she fired back at the manager. Marchand's brow twisted in a scowl, and he thrust an accusatory finger towards the diamond necklace adorning Sofia's neck.

The princess's hand snapped up to cover the jewels, her expression hardening. Elizabeth watched, transfixed, as the confrontation unfolded.

Princess Sofia spun on her heel. Her steps, brisk and charged with frustration, she almost collided with Elizabeth, surprise flashing across her face before she quickly masked it behind a practiced smile.

"Elizabeth." The princess's smile remained fixed, though her eyes still flickered with irritation. "It seems the caller has disappeared." She gave a small, dismissive wave. "As I'd suspected, nothing of consequence."

Elizabeth's eyes followed Sofia's fingers as they brushed the glittering diamonds at her throat. Each gemstone caught the light, casting tiny rainbows on the princess's porcelain skin.

Elizabeth leaned in slightly, her voice tinged with genuine admiration. "Your necklace is exquisite. Is it a family heirloom?"

"It belonged to my great-grandmother and is one of my favourite pieces." Sofia slipped her hand through Elizabeth's arm, steering her back towards the dining room.

Elizabeth glanced over her shoulder and saw Monsieur Marchand still rooted to the spot. His eyes narrowed. The intensity of his earlier exchange with the princess was highly irregular between an employee and someone of her rank. This breach of decorum gnawed at Elizabeth, making her question the true nature of their relationship.

Princess Sofia leaned in, her eyes sparkling with curiosity. "Now, Elizabeth, tell me all about the earl."

Caught off guard by the princess's words, it took Elizabeth a moment to register the way Sofia had referred to Alexander as "the earl." The use of Alexander's title struck her as odd, since only minutes earlier, Sofia had addressed him by his Christian name as if they were old friends. Questions swirled in her mind: did the princess's interest lie in the man or the title?

While Sofia's charm was undeniable, her ability to switch personas was troubling, reminding Elizabeth of a chameleon – a rare, exotic lizard she had encountered on archaeological digs with her father in Egypt. It had the ability to change its colours to blend in, hiding its true self in plain sight.

Was the princess as fickle as quicksilver, shifting her persona to suit her needs? Or had Elizabeth's recent adventures made her overly suspicious, seeing deceit and treachery where none existed?

Chapter Four

E LIZABETH SWEPT INTO HER suite, her inky locks tousled and her cheeks glowing from the afternoon's lively mixed doubles tennis match with Monsieur Jacques Renault. A hint of triumph danced in her hazel eyes, recalling the thrill of their competitive teamwork on the court.

Monsieur Renault, a Parisian jeweller, with his sturdy, athletic frame and slicked-back dark hair threaded with silver, cut an imposing figure as he readied himself at the net. Their serendipitous partnership bloomed on the court, with Elizabeth seamlessly synchronising with Renault's game.

Her movements were feline in their quickness, her eyes tracking the ball's trajectory, intercepting volleys and placing returns with tactical precision. In contrast, Renault's powerful serves and blistering smashes overwhelmed their opponents, his experience and strength on full display. Each strategic exchange and hard-fought point showcased Elizabeth's instincts and Renault's mastery.

The final scoreline of 6-4, 7-5 echoed the seamless harmony of their teamwork, each victory celebrated with shared glances of triumph. As they left the court, the spark in Elizabeth's eyes and the subtle curve of Renault's lips hinted at a growing respect between the victorious duo.

Elizabeth crossed to the en-suite bathroom. Pausing before the mirror, she cupped her hands beneath the tap, splashing cool water onto her flushed cheeks. The invigorating sensation drew a soft sigh from her lips, and she lingered for a moment, relishing the coolness as it soothed her overheated skin. Shrugging off her sweat-dampened tennis whites, she allowed them to pool at her feet before placing them in the basket.

Back in the bedroom, she threw open the wardrobe doors, her eyes scanning the array of dresses. A peach-coloured frock caught her attention, its puffed sleeves and flowing A-line skirt a welcome departure from her tennis attire. She reached for the dress, the light chiffon cool against her still-heated skin.

At the vanity, Elizabeth leaned forward, studying her reflection. A few deft swipes of rose-pink lipstick across her lips and a quick brush through her tangled hair transformed her from the fierce competitor on the court to a picture of elegance. She reached for the bottle of orange blossom perfume, dabbing the floral fragrance on her wrists, the smell evoking memories of her *yiayia's* garden and the many happy holidays she'd spent in Greece.

With a final appraising glance in the mirror, Elizabeth gathered her things, her steps light as she hurried to meet Aunt Beatrice in the hotel lounge.

The lift chimed, and Elizabeth stepped into the lobby, her eyes scanning the expanse. She glanced at her wristwatch, a small smile playing on her lips as she pictured Meli, racket in hand, partaking in her tennis lesson.

She crossed the foyer, approaching the reception desk where Monsieur Marchand appeared engrossed in paperwork.

His head lifted as she neared, his face brightening as he slid the papers he'd been working on beneath the visitor's book. Monsieur Marchand inclined his head. "Lady Hawthorne, I trust your tennis match was enjoyable this afternoon?"

Elizabeth's expression softened. "It was, Monsieur." She leaned forward slightly, as if sharing a secret. "We were quite the dynamic duo on the court."

Marchand's eyebrows shot up, his interest piqued. "Oh? That sounds like a formidable pairing. How did you fare?"

A hint of amusement danced in Elizabeth's eyes. "We won. His skill with the racket is quite impressive. Keeping up with him was a challenge."

The hotelier chuckled. "Yes, Monsieur Renault is very competitive."

"He certainly is." She took a step back, her gaze drifting towards the lounge. "If you'll excuse me, monsieur, I shouldn't keep my aunt waiting. She's a stickler for punctuality."

Marchand's smile was understanding. "Of course. Enjoy the rest of your day, Lady Hawthorne."

With a parting glance, Elizabeth turned on her heel and made her way towards the lounge.

Pausing as she entered, Elizabeth's gaze landed on Aunt Beatrice and Evelyn, locked in a fierce bridge battle against Mrs Hicks and Mr Gray. Evelyn, usually so timid, had transformed into a sharp-eyed strategist, her fingers expertly flipping the cards.

The room buzzed with polite conversation, but beneath the cordial smiles, tension simmered. Aunt Beatrice's posture was stiff, her lips a mere line, her eyes laser-focused on the card table. Opposite her, Mrs Hicks matched her intensity, her knuckles white as she clutched her cards, determination etched into every line of her face.

Elizabeth navigated the room, offering warm glances and nods to the other guests. As she neared the table, Aunt Beatrice's eyebrow arched in silent inquiry, her eyes never leaving the cards.

"Apologies for my tardiness." Elizabeth's smile brightened as she slid into the empty wingback chair beside Alexander. "I ran into Monsieur Marchand in the reception; he wanted to know all about my match with Monsieur Renault."

A flicker of fear flashed in Alexander's eyes, but he masked it swiftly. "And how did you fare on the court?"

A look of triumph crossed Elizabeth's face. "We won." She angled her body towards him before continuing. "Monsieur Renault is utterly relentless on the court, though I flatter myself that I kept up."

Monsieur Renault materialised at Elizabeth's elbow, as if summoned by her words. His smooth Parisian accent adding a layer of charm to his words. "You are too modest, Lady Elizabeth." A chuckle rumbled in his throat, a roguish grin tugging at his lips.

Elizabeth turned, her mouth opening to make the introductions, when recognition danced across Renault's features as his gaze landed on Alexander. For a heartbeat, the two men's eyes locked - a fleeting, silent communication passing between them.

Alexander gave the slightest imperceptible shake of his head, and just like that, the moment passed. Renault's expression shuttered, his affable mask sliding back into place.

"Monsieur Renault," Alexander dipped his chin in a polite gesture, his tone remaining cordial. "A pleasure to make your acquaintance."

Renault extended his hand. "The pleasure is all mine, Lord Cavendish." As their palms met, Elizabeth couldn't help but wonder how Renault knew who Alexander was, without any need for an introduction. Their exchange seemed to have an air of performance about it, as if the rules of some mysterious game were being carefully adhered to.

She motioned to the vacant chair. "Please, Monsieur Renault. Won't you join us?"

Renault bowed his head in acknowledgment and sank into the proffered seat.

Beside her, Alexander picked at a loose thread on the arm of his chair, his gaze constantly flickering towards the entrance. Elizabeth leaned in, her eyes keenly observing the tension between the two men. "And what brings you to Cannes, Monsieur Renault?" She infused her voice with a light, curious tone, aiming to dispel the unease. "Is it purely for pleasure?"

"Mostly business." Renault's smile curved with a subtle, conspiratorial edge, his voice lowering to a confiding murmur. "Although, I always make time to enjoy the ... amenities on offer." His gaze strayed towards the nearby cluster of chaises, where several sun-bronzed ladies reclined on the sun terrace.

Elizabeth raised an eyebrow, a playful smile on her lips. "And is there a Madame Renault who shares in these travels?"

Renault chuckled. "No, my work consumes most of my time. Many of my clients insist I travel to them; it helps maintain their privacy." He cleared his throat, shifting his focus back to Elizabeth. "Discretion is paramount in my profession." His dark eyes conveyed steady confidence. "And I always guard my clients' privacy, whatever the cost."

For a fleeting moment, she couldn't shake the feeling that Renault's words carried a reassuring undercurrent - as if they were aimed at Alexander.

But she quickly brushed the peculiar notion aside. Surely she was letting her imagination get the better of her. Perhaps her earlier exertion had left her feeling a little lightheaded.

Renault's gaze flicked towards Alexander before he continued, his tone unruffled. "The auction tomorrow will no doubt attract interest from society's more ... elite. Which I find perfect for forging new alliances. So it's as you English would say..." He gave a faint smile. "Killing two birds with one stone?"

A sharp commotion between a well-dressed, middle-aged gentleman and a young waiter drew Elizabeth's attention. The older man's expression betrayed unrestrained irritation as he gesticulated animatedly. Elizabeth couldn't help but feel a pang of sympathy for the poor waiter, no doubt powerless to object for fear of losing his position.

With a disdainful flick of his hand, the gentleman dismissed the flustered waiter, his cool gaze scanning the room before settling on Alexander. A subtle nod passed between the two men, and then Alexander leapt up from his seat.

"If you'll excuse me." Alexander avoided Elizabeth's inquisitive gaze. "I, er, need to..." With a terse nod, he turned on his heel and strode towards the newcomer, conferring with him in hushed tones.

Elizabeth watched Alexander's departure, her curiosity piqued. She turned back to Renault, gesturing towards the two men. "Do you know who that gentleman is, the one Lord Cavendish is speaking with?"

Renault followed her line of sight, his expression calm. "That is Monsieur Felix Bouchér – he is in charge of tomorrow's auction." His gaze flicked back to Elizabeth, a spark of knowing in his eyes.

Her mind churned, trying to connect the pieces. What manner of business could Alexander possibly have with the organiser of tomorrow's auction?

Meli breezed into the lounge, drawing Elizabeth's attention from her thoughts. A faint flush from her tennis lesson still coloured her cheeks. Her face lit up as she spotted her cousin. "Elizabeth!" She waved. "I met Miss Hicks on the tennis courts. We shared a lesson, though I must confess her skills far surpass mine."

Clara smiled warmly, inclining her head slightly. "Hardly. Your cousin kept me on my toes."

Elizabeth's smile widened, a fondness in her expression as she watched her lively cousin. "Meli seems to have an endless reserve of energy, doesn't she? Enough to power all of Cannes, I daresay."

A triumphant cry from the card table rang out as Aunt Beatrice and Evelyn rose, smug satisfaction etched on their faces.

Mrs Hicks pushed back from the table, her lips pressed into a thin line. "Well played, Lady Hawthorne, Miss Brown." She levelled a pointed glare at Mr Gray. "Perhaps we should swap partners for the rematch – Miss Brown and I against you and Mr Gray."

Aunt Beatrice arched a brow, a faint smile playing at her lips. "Now, now, my dear Mrs Hicks, there's no need to be such a poor loser.

Bridge can be a rather complex game, even for those with a head for strategy." She gave a delicate tsk, the corner of her mouth quirking upwards. "But with enough practice, I'm sure you'll grasp the fundamentals ... eventually."

Mr Gray chuckled, shaking his head. "It seems I'm the one in need of practice. Perhaps we should consider a different game next time, one where I might stand a better chance? Perhaps even a friendly wager to make it more interesting."

Aunt Beatrice's smile faded, her tone firm. "Most certainly not." She paused, her expression softening. "However, I'd be delighted if you could join us tomorrow evening for an opera gala. It promises to be quite the event."

Her eyes shifted to Mrs Hicks, and she offered a tight-lipped smile. "Of course, you and your daughter are welcome to join us." She glanced down, adjusting an already neatly stacked deck of cards. "But I must warn you, opera isn't for everyone."

Mrs Hicks's gaze swept over Aunt Beatrice with exaggerated disinterest. "I dare say there are those who will find this local event quite…"

She paused, her eyes glinting with veiled condescension as she gave a delicate, dismissive flick of her wrist. "entertaining. But after watching Rosa Ponselle perform at the Metropolitan last month, I think Clara and I will find it rather lacking."

Aunt Beatrice's lips tightened into a disapproving line. She turned to Mr Gray. "I hope you're not too grand to attend our little event, Mr Gray?"

"Well ... I, er," Mr Gray cleared his throat, shifting uncomfortably in his seat.

A faint, satisfied smile played on Beatrice's lips as she turned to regard Mrs Hicks. "It's a charity event, in aid of a good cause, and my nephew, Lord Cavendish, will be with us. Not to mention the charming Princess Sofia de' Medici."

Mrs Hicks's eyes narrowed at the mention of the princess, a trace of hostility flickering over her expression before she composed herself, a reaction that didn't go unnoticed by Elizabeth.

The hesitation melted from Gray's features instantly, a subtle shift in his demeanour that did not go unnoticed by Elizabeth. "Well then, if it's for charity, how can I refuse?" His voice took on a warm, genial note. "The work of the great Enrico Caruso has long been a personal favourite of mine. Will he be performing?"

At Mr Gray's mention of Caruso, a ripple of confusion spread through the group. Elizabeth's brow furrowed as she exchanged a perplexed glance with Evelyn. Aunt Beatrice arched an eyebrow. "I do hope not, Mr Gray, as the renowned Caruso passed away in 1921."

Gray cleared his throat, a faint flush creeping up his neck. "Ah yes, of course. What was I thinking? My brain must still be addled from the journey."

As the group dispersed, Elizabeth's gaze lingered on Mr Gray, her mind churning. For a fleeting moment, she had been certain he would decline Aunt Beatrice's invitation - his initial hesitation had been palpable. And yet, in the span of a heartbeat, that reluctance had melted away, replaced by an overly eager enthusiasm that struck Elizabeth as deeply incongruous.

What could have prompted such an abrupt about-face? The claim that it was for charity? Or was there something else, some hidden motivation, that lay beneath the surface?

Surely, no true opera aficionado could be unaware of the great Enrico Caruso's passing?

Chapter Five

THE HAWTHORNE PARTY TOOK their seats at the breakfast table in Le Jardin Matin. Around them, the room buzzed with the lively discourse of diners savouring their breakfast. French doors framed the garden view, where palm trees swayed and vibrant splashes of lavender and bougainvillea coloured the lush greenery. The aromas of rich espresso and freshly baked croissants filled the air, complemented by the crisp, salty breeze from the Mediterranean.

Aunt Beatrice eyed Alexander over the rim of her teacup, her brows knitting into a sharp arch. "Alexander, dear, how is your acquaintance with the princess progressing? I hope things are moving in the right direction?"

Alexander stirred his coffee, the spoon clinking against the cup with a hesitant rhythm. He glanced up briefly before looking away. "We dined at La Belle époque, then went to a casino." The words fell flat.

Aunt Beatrice's teacup met the saucer with a muted clatter. Her lips pressed into a thin line. "A casino?" She drummed her fingers against the table, each beat carrying her disapproval. "Really, Alexander ... I hope you haven't inherited your late father's penchant for gambling. Such indulgences led the Wexford estate to its current precarious state."

Alexander shifted in his seat, his fingers tightening around the handle of his cup. "I can assure you, Aunt, it wasn't my choice to go there. I observed more than I participated."

Elizabeth watched from across the table, noting the strain that tightened Alexander's features, the way his eyes didn't quite meet anyone's, darting away as if seeking an escape.

Aunt Beatrice pressed on. "And will you be seeing the princess this morning?"

Alexander fiddled with the edge of his napkin, folding and unfolding the crisp linen. "I have some personal matters to attend to today."

Aunt Beatrice leaned forward, curiosity and challenge mixing in her eyes. "Personal matters? And what could be more pressing than securing a promising connection with the princess?"

Alexander's shoulders tensed. Before he could respond, Elizabeth reached for a croissant and tore off a piece. "I believe the princess prefers to start her day later."

Gratitude flickered across Alexander's face, his eyes meeting Elizabeth's for a fleeting moment – a silent thank you communicated in a shared glance.

Aunt Beatrice huffed, her disapproval evident. "Very well, Alexander. But remember, your responsibilities should always come first."

Alexander straightened in his seat, his voice low and strained as he addressed Aunt Beatrice. "I'm well aware of my responsibilities," he asserted. "And as I've already told you, I'm taking steps to deal with my situation. Now, can we please change the subject?"

Aunt Beatrice's eyebrows shot up, her teacup pausing mid-air as she registered his tone. Elizabeth, equally taken aback, stared at her cousin. It was rare for Alexander, usually so mild-mannered, to stand up to Aunt Beatrice .

Alexander's outburst left a palpable tension in the air. Elizabeth's gaze darted between her cousin and aunt before settling on Aunt Beatrice. "Aunt, how do you and Evelyn plan to spend the day since you don't want to join Meli and I on our shopping trip?"

Aunt Beatrice's fork clinked against her plate as she set it down. She smoothed her napkin, her eyes distant. "The opera this evening is quite enough excitement for one day." Her gaze sharpened, a hint of curiosity in her voice. "Though I hear there's a Sargent at today's auction. Perhaps a brief appearance wouldn't hurt."

Alexander's fingers tightened around his coffee cup. He set it down with a sharp clink, leaning forward. "Aunt, surely you'd prefer afternoon tea at the Carlton?" His eyes flicked to Evelyn. "It's far too lovely a day to be cooped up indoors. Evelyn should join us, of course."

Elizabeth noticed the slight furrow in her aunt's brow as she considered Alexander's suggestion.

Aunt Beatrice paused, her demeanour softening as she considered Alexander's proposal. A gentle smile curved her lips. "Afternoon tea does sound lovely, especially since the Carlton serves such excellent fare."

She turned to Evelyn. "Evelyn, what do you say to tea at the Carlton?"

Evelyn's face lit up, her smile widening. "That does sound delightful, Lord Cavendish."

Satisfied with the consensus, Aunt Beatrice nodded her approval. "Very well, Alexander, you've convinced us. It'll be a delightful way to spend the afternoon, far better than a crowded auction room."

Alexander stood, smoothing his jacket as he reached for the morning paper. A relieved smile spread across his face as he nodded. "Splendid. I'll go make the arrangements now."

Alexander hurried off to make the arrangements. Aunt Beatrice rose, her fingers smoothing the creases from her maroon dress. She glanced toward the gardens, gesturing to Evelyn. "Shall we take a turn around the gardens?" Her eyes lingered on the lush blooms visible from the breakfast room. "They are particularly lovely at this time of year."

Before departing, she turned to Elizabeth and Meli. "And remember, girls, the curtain waits for no one." Her sharp gaze underscoring the importance of her words.

Elizabeth nodded. "Of course, Aunt."

As Elizabeth and Meli exited the breakfast room, Clara caught Meli's eye and beckoned with a broad, welcoming smile.

Meli's face brightened as they approached the Hicks's table, her hands clasping together in delight. "Clara, Mrs Hicks, how lovely to see you again."

Mrs Hicks tilted her head playfully, resting her chin on her hand, a twinkle in her eye. "And where are you two young ladies hurrying off to this morning?"

"We're planning a shopping trip along the Boulevard de Croisette," Meli leaned in, her eyes bright with excitement. "Would you care to join us?"

Mrs Hicks shook her head, her diamond earrings catching the sunlight. "Not this time, thank you. We're saving all our energy for tonight. Besides, Clara and I had more than our fill of shopping in Paris." A small, satisfied smile played at the corners of her lips. "I dare say there was hardly a dress or pair of shoes to be had by the time we'd finished."

She gave Clara an affectionate pat on the arm. "But if it makes my little girl happy, then who am I to deny her?"

Elizabeth, drawn into the conversation, asked, "Do you have something special planned?"

Mrs Hicks swept her hands through the air with a theatrical flourish, her gold bracelets jingling. "Absolutely. We're starting with dinner and dancing at *La Rotonde*, then it's on to the casino for a flutter."

Meli responded, her voice tinged with longing. "Sounds like a thrilling evening."

"Well, it's only money, after all, and you can't take it with you, can you?" Mrs Hicks laughed, her carefree sound filling the air.

Meli mustered a smile, though her eyes betrayed a wisp of envy. "That sounds like such fun."

Elizabeth smiled as they prepared to depart. "We shall look forward to hearing all about it tomorrow. Come Meli, we ought to press on; the boutiques along Boulevard de Croisette beckon."

Mrs Hicks flicked a glance at the wall clock. "And so does Collette." She rose, draining her teacup as she signalled Clara to follow. "Come along, Clara, we mustn't dally."

"Enjoy your shopping trip," she called over her shoulder as they headed to their appointment at the hotel salon.

Meli let out an audible sigh as she watched them leave. The longing in her gaze lingering on their departing figures.

Elizabeth squeezed Meli's arm, a mix of comfort and concern in her touch. She knew all too well her cousin's craving for excitement. It had once led her to stow away aboard the SS Andromeda, entangling her in a ghastly murder. The memory still sent a chill through Elizabeth.

Taking a steadying breath, she pushed her fears aside. "Ready?"

Meli's nod was almost imperceptible, her gaze flicking to the floor.

"Is your heart set on the Boulevard?" Elizabeth asked, tilting her head slightly, watching Meli's reaction closely.

Meli glanced sideways, curiosity piqued. "How do you mean?"

"Well," Elizabeth continued, a mischievous glint in her eye, "how would you like to see the real Cannes? Away from the path trodden by the more … well-heeled?"

Meli's eyes widened, her excitement palpable. "Oh, Elizabeth, I would adore that!" She clapped her hands together, unable to contain her enthusiasm.

"Then shall we?" Elizabeth linked her arm through Meli's, guiding her towards the exit. "But not a word to Aunt Beatrice," she added with a conspiratorial wink.

As they strode past The Grand Hall, where staff bustled about preparing for the auction, Elizabeth's gaze was irresistibly drawn inside. At the centre of the room stood Alexander, his posture tense as he gestured. Opposite him, Felix Bouchér, with placating hands and a calm demeanour, appeared to be trying to temper the situation.

Elizabeth felt a twinge of concern. The memory of how abruptly Alexander had excused himself to speak with Monsieur Bouchér – secretive, almost urgent – had sparked her suspicions. Seeing the intensity of their exchange now only deepened her worry.

Meli glanced sideways at her cousin, sensing the gears turning in Elizabeth's mind. "A penny for your thoughts, Elizabeth?"

Elizabeth offered a small smile, her brow furrowed in contemplation. "It's Alexander. His arrival in Cannes is puzzling. He's been evasive about why he's here, and I've never known him to take a holiday in such a place, nor does he have apparent business interests here." She paused, her thoughts coalescing into concern.

Meli's eyes widened, her curiosity piqued. "That is unusual. Do you think something's amiss?"

Elizabeth sighed. "I'm beginning to think so. His behaviour has changed; snapping at Aunt

Beatrice was so unlike him. And there was that odd moment between him and Renault yesterday – I was sure Renault recognised him, but Alexander behaved as if they were strangers. His discussions with Monsieur Bouchér have only added to my suspicions. There's a tension around him lately that's hard to ignore."

Meli paused, pondering a moment before venturing a guess. "Do you think it could be Aunt Beatrice's matchmaking that's unsettling him? The idea of being pushed down the aisle with the princess might be weighing on him."

Elizabeth gave a slight nod, her eyes softening as she gazed into the distance, contemplating. "I'm sure that's adding to his stress. While Aunt Beatrice's methods can be overbearing, her heart is in the right place. She's deeply concerned about Alexander's financial woes and sees this alliance with the princess as a practical solution. But I can't help thinking there's something more to it."

They stepped out of the hotel, leaving the chic boutiques and *patisseries* behind. Steering away from the main tourist path, Elizabeth led Meli down a narrow alley that revealed a layer of Cannes seldom seen by outsiders. Here, the city's authentic heart beat – a lattice of backstreets adorned with faded shutters and peeling paint, each telling stories of everyday struggles and simple joys.

Artisanal shops proudly displayed their crafts, while market stalls burst with vivid blooms, fresh fruits and vegetables, the air resonant with robust local dialects. Cosy cafés spilled the rich aromas of brewed coffee and baked goods into the alley, beckoning passersby to linger.

They wove through the crowd, completely absorbed by the charm of this hidden slice of the city, a stark contrast to the elegant hotels and affluent areas they had just left.

Meli's eyes widened as they passed a fragrant flower stand. She took a deep breath, visibly relaxed and enchanted. "This place is wonderful, Elizabeth! How did you ever find it?"

Elizabeth chuckled, her eyes twinkling with a hint of mischief. "Quite by chance. Caroline and I were a little adventurous while shopping last year and stumbled upon this charming area after getting lost. We didn't tell Aunt Beatrice, of course; she would have been quite horrified knowing we'd visited such a place unchaperoned."

Meli laughed, her delight echoing off the old stone walls. "It's like stepping into another world," she mused, absorbing the relaxed ambiance.

Elizabeth nodded in agreement, her hands gesturing broadly as if to encompass their surroundings. "Yes, it's quite remarkable how different this Cannes is from the one the wealthy tourists see. Perhaps Alexander, too, is caught between two worlds, not unlike these contrasting parts of town."

"How do you mean?" Meli asked, her forehead creasing in curiosity.

"Duty and expectation dictate his destiny to preserve the family title and estate, whereas I have a feeling Alexander's heart is pulling him in the opposite direction."

"You think Alexander's heart has already been claimed? But who?" Meli's voice rose slightly with surprise.

"I do indeed, and I'm certain the recipient of his affections is Miss Hicks," Elizabeth revealed, her voice lowering to a conspiratorial whisper.

"Speaking of the princess..." Meli nudged Elizabeth, nodding discreetly towards the elegant figure striding ahead of them. "Isn't that her over there?"

Princess Sofia's hurried steps faltered on the uneven cobblestones, her frequent glances over her shoulder betraying a palpable unease. "She looks distressed, almost as if she's fleeing from someone," Meli observed.

Scanning the surroundings, Elizabeth's attention snagged on a man lingering at the corner, his well-tailored attire and black fedora adorned with a peacock feather incongruous among the less affluent locals. Meli leaned closer, her voice a hushed murmur as her fingers tightened on Elizabeth's arm. "Do you think he's following her?"

Keeping her eyes fixed on the man, Elizabeth furrowed her brow, the concern evident in her voice. "I'm uncertain, but women like Princess Sofia often attract unwanted attention."

As if sensing their scrutiny, Princess Sofia cast a final, furtive look over her shoulder before darting into a nearby café.

Meli's eyes narrowed, a determined set to her jaw. "Do you think we should follow her, just in case?"

Elizabeth nodded, her mind already charting their course. "If I remember correctly, this café has a side entrance. Let's make our way there, in case the princess tries to slip out that way." They altered their route, keeping the grey-haired man in their peripheral vision while trying to remain inconspicuous.

As they turned into a quieter alley, the sounds of the bustling streets grew muted, replaced by the echo of their own footsteps. Elizabeth quickened her pace, Meli staying close, her eyes darting nervously around.

Princess Sofia appeared from a doorway, her eyes wide and her hand clutching a small perfume atomiser like a makeshift weapon. "Why are you following me?" she demanded, her voice sharp with fear and suspicion.

Elizabeth and Meli froze mid-step, raising their hands in a calming gesture.

Recognition dawned in Sofia's eyes as she lowered the bottle, her shoulders sagging with relief. "Elizabeth, Meli ... I'm sorry, I've been a little on edge lately."

Meli stepped forward, her concern evident. "Is everything all right? We thought you seemed ... distressed."

Sofia glanced back before turning to them, her voice low and urgent. "We can't talk here," she replied, motioning towards the café entrance.

Elizabeth nodded, understanding the need for discretion. "Of course. I noticed another café near here. We can talk there."

They made their way to a small café tucked away in a side street. The quaint outdoor seating area, shaded by large umbrellas, exuded an air of quiet charm. Inside, polished wooden tables and a counter displaying an array of freshly baked pastries gave the place an elegant simplicity.

They chose a secluded table at the back, away from prying eyes. As they settled in, Sofia's anxiety became more apparent. Her hands trembled as she clutched her purse, eyes darting around the room, searching for hidden dangers.

When the waiter arrived with their order, Elizabeth poured each of them a cup of tea, trying to offer a semblance of normalcy. She watched Sofia's fingers fidget with the cup's handle, her knuckles turning white. Elizabeth leaned closer, her voice low and soothing as she offered reassurance, "Princess Sofia, you seem very distressed. Whatever it is, you can trust us."

Sofia took a shuddering breath, eyes glistening. "There's a man," she whispered. "He's been following me. I first noticed him in Cote d'Azur. I thought I had escaped him when I came to Cannes, but it seems he has found me again."

Meli's brow furrowed as she placed a comforting hand on Sofia's. "Who is he? Why is he following you?"

Sofia hesitated, a tear sliding down her cheek. She brushed it away with a shaking hand. "I wasn't entirely honest with you last night. The reason I came here is because I am fleeing a broken engagement. My fiancé ... he's a dangerous man with dubious connections." Her voice cracked as she lowered her gaze. "When I broke off our engagement, he was furious. I fled to the south of France to escape him, but now it seems he has sent someone to bring me back... I'm frightened for my life."

Elizabeth and Meli exchanged shocked glances. Concern etching her features, Elizabeth placed a comforting hand on Sofia's trembling arm, feeling the coiled tension under her fingertips. "Have you been to the police?"

Sofia shook her head, tears spilling down her cheeks. "He has connections everywhere. I don't know who I can trust."

"Even in the police?" Meli's eyes widened.

Sofia nodded, a shudder running through her body. "Especially in the police," she confided.

Elizabeth's voice dropped to a hushed, urgent whisper as she addressed Sofia, ensuring their conversation remained private. "I understand your fear, but if you explain your situation to the police, they can protect you."

Sofia's eyes widened, a flash of panic crossing her features. She shook her head, her hands gripping the edge of her purse. "I can't risk it, Elizabeth. His influence stretches far and wide.

If he finds out I've spoken to them, it could put everyone in danger, including you and Meli."

Meli reached across the table, her fingertips brushing Sofia's in a gentle, reassuring gesture. "But you can't keep running forever. There has to be a way to ensure your safety."

Sofia took a deep breath, her expression shifting from fear to determination. She straightened her back and squared her shoulders, a steely resolve settling over her. "This is my burden to bear." Her tone remained steady despite the weight of her words. "I appreciate your concern, but I will deal with it on my own terms."

Elizabeth watched as the princess regained her composure with surprising swiftness. The transformation was impressive, almost too seamless. A flicker of doubt crept into Elizabeth's mind. How could someone so visibly shaken moments ago now seem so calm?

Was it just resilience born of necessity?

Or was there something more at play here?

Chapter Six

Princess Sofia's resolve to attend the opera surprised Elizabeth, given the harrowing incident mere hours before. Despite Elizabeth's advice to maintain a low profile, Sofia refused to hide away. The sudden shift – from the trembling, terrified woman in the café to this confident figure – left Elizabeth puzzled. Was it genuine bravery or something more? She chastised herself for her ungenerous thoughts, yet a niggling sense of unease persisted, like a whisper in the back of her mind that refused to be silenced.

The last of the dinner guests filtered out of the dining room as the grand foyer of Le Majestique filled with a subtle buzz of evening plans being set into motion. Aunt Beatrice, her midnight blue gown catching the light with each impatient shift, tapped her bejewelled fingers against her clutch. "Really, the princess might be of royal blood, but this tardiness is a most unseemly display? And now, Mr Gray has sent word he's been detained and will meet us at the theatre. It seems no one values punctuality these days."

Beside her, Evelyn's soft lavender frock rustled as she turned, her voice a hushed murmur meant to soothe her employer. "I'm sure she just wants to ensure she looks her best, Lady Beatrice."

Aunt Beatrice's lips pressed into a thin line. "Be that as it may, this lack of consideration is most vexing."

Elizabeth, the delicate beadwork of her pale blue chiffon Jeanne Lanvin gown sparkling beneath the chandeliers, laid a comforting hand on her aunt's forearm. "I'm sure she'll be down soon," she reassured, her eyes briefly meeting Aunt Beatrice's before scanning the thinning crowd. "And I'm quite certain Mr Gray wouldn't delay without good cause."

Across the foyer, Alexander engaged in animated conversation with Mrs Hicks and her daughter, Clara. Elizabeth observed the earl's demeanour soften, his posture relaxed, and his laughter genuine – so different from his stiff, awkward interactions with Princess Sofia.

Aunt Beatrice's gaze fixed on Alexander, her fingers tightening around her clutch. She watched the easy camaraderie between the earl and the Hicks women, a clear affront to the match she had hoped to orchestrate with the regal princess.

Meli, in a vibrant jade-green dress with a dropped waist and swirling skirt, fidgeted beside Elizabeth. "Do you think she's changed her mind?"

Silence fell over the grand foyer as Princess Sofia appeared at the top of the staircase, commanding every eye in the room. She paused there, letting the moment linger, her golden hair cascading in soft waves that framed her delicate features.

Elizabeth's brow furrowed as she studied the princess. This poised, self-assured woman bore little resemblance to the trembling figure from hours earlier. Sofia's eyes no longer held a haunted look and instead exuded a confidence that contradicted her earlier distress.

Sofia descended the stairs, her steps deliberate. The champagne silk of Sofia's gown caught the light, but it was the jewellery that demanded attention.

An intricate diamond necklace rested on Sofia's collarbone, its large oval stones scattering prismatic reflections across her face. From her ears, cascades of smaller diamonds swayed with each step, drawing Elizabeth's eye.

Alexander's expression remained coolly impassive, betraying none of the captivation Aunt Beatrice had hoped to inspire.

Meli leaned in close to Elizabeth, her eyes sparkling with admiration. "Well, she certainly knows how to make an entrance, doesn't she?"

Elizabeth pressed her lips together, her unease mirroring the tension in Alexander's posture. "She does indeed," she murmured, her gaze flicking back to the princess.

Aunt Beatrice's lips curved into a satisfied smile as Sofia reached the bottom of the stairs. "Good of you to join us. Finally."

Sofia's eyes swept over the group with a confident, almost imperious air, oblivious to Aunt Beatrice's sharp tone. She paused, looking expectantly at Alexander. "Shall we?"

Alexander's jaw tightened as he extended his arm to Sofia. Her fingers curled around his sleeve, a subtle triumph in her smile. His eyes met Clara's across the room, a flicker of regret passing between them. Clara's smile faltered, but she quickly regained her composure, lifting her chin defiantly.

As Alexander led Sofia towards the exit, Clara's gaze followed them. Her usual animated chatter ceased, replaced by an uncharacteristic stillness, her knuckles turning white as her grip tightened on the stem of her champagne glass.

Elizabeth's heart went out to both her cousin and Miss Hicks, their unspoken emotions clear in that fleeting look. Her attention snapped to Mrs. Hicks. The older woman's eyes followed the departing couple with undisguised contempt, her gaze narrowing to slits as she fixed Sofia with an icy, withering glare. The sheer malevolence in Mrs. Hicks' gaze could have wilted every flower in Le Majestique's garden.

"Elizabeth, do stop dawdling!" Aunt Beatrice's voice pierced the air. "We mustn't keep everyone waiting."

As the group made their way to the Rolls-Royce waiting for them in front of the hotel, Elizabeth couldn't shake the feeling of unease. The brief journey to the Théâtre du Boulevard did little to calm her nerves. In a matter of minutes, the magnificent façade of the theatre loomed before them as Victor, Le Majestique's chauffeur, brought the car to a smooth stop. He stepped out and opened the rear door with practiced efficiency.

Princess Sofia emerged first, her champagne silk gown shimmering beneath the streetlamps as she alighted. Alexander followed, his usually confident stride slightly hesitant. He adjusted his bowtie, his fingers betraying a hint of nervousness.

Aunt Beatrice lingered by the motorcar under the guise of adjusting her shawl. "Evelyn, dear, could you assist me for a moment? I feel the evening chill setting in." Her tone was casual, yet pointed as her gaze flickered toward Alexander and the princess. "Alexander, why don't you escort Princess Sofia inside? We wouldn't want her to catch a cold in this breeze."

Alexander's eyes darkened momentarily, his fingers curling into his palms. Drawing in a controlled breath, he squared his shoulders, masking his reluctance with a polite smile. "Of course, Aunt." He extended his arm to Sofia, who took it with a beguiling smile, her gloved hand resting lightly on his sleeve. As they led the way towards the theatre, Alexander's steps were measured, his posture straight but rigid – a noticeable contrast to Sofia's effortless poise.

With her shawl now satisfactorily draped around her shoulders, Aunt Beatrice signalled the others to proceed, deliberately maintaining a distance that allowed Alexander and Sofia a semblance of privacy.

Meli leaned toward Elizabeth, her voice low with concern as she watched their retreating backs. "Oh, Elizabeth, he seems so desperately uncomfortable, doesn't he?" Her eyes remained fixed on Alexander's rigid posture.

Elizabeth nodded, her gaze tracking the pair until they disappeared inside the grand entrance. "It's all becoming too much for him."

She kept her voice hushed. "Aunt Beatrice's schemes are clearly taking their toll, but he's too much of a gentleman to let his true feelings show."

As they entered the grand foyer of the Théâtre du Boulevard, Princess Sofia's eyes sparkled with excitement. "Why don't we have a drink before the performance begins?" she suggested, her melodic voice carrying a hint of invitation. "It'll be the perfect way to kick off the evening."

Aunt Beatrice hesitated, disapproval flickering across her face, but she nodded, keen to curry favour with the princess. The group settled into a cosy nook at the elegant cocktail bar, where soft lighting created a warm ambiance around the polished mahogany surfaces and plush velvet chairs.

"Evelyn and I will have tonic water." She met the waiter's gaze firmly, daring anyone to object.

Princess Sofia leaned in to Meli, a spark of mischief in her grin. "Meli, won't you join me in a cocktail?" Her voice was light, inviting.

Meli glanced at Elizabeth, her hands fidgeting with the edge of her clutch. "I'm only eighteen; I'm too young to indulge." Disappointment laced her voice.

The princess waved a dismissive hand, her bracelets jingling. "In France, the legal age is sixteen," she whispered conspiratorially. "Let me see ... a Mary Pickford will be perfect for you."

Meli turned to Aunt Beatrice, seeking approval. The matriarch sighed, her expression stern. "Very well, just this once. But don't make a habit of it."

Sofia turned to Elizabeth. "And for you, Elizabeth?"

Elizabeth angled her head slightly, her smile warm. "I'll stick with an iced tea, thank you."

"And I'll have a—"

"Champs-Élysées, with a twist of Meyer lemon." The unexpected voice turned every head at the table.

Princess Sofia's eyes widened before her expression hardened, her posture straightening with irritation.

Elizabeth's eyebrows arched when Alexander ordered a neat whisky, an unusual choice for him so early in the evening. Aunt Beatrice's lips thinned as she tapped her fingers on the table, each tap sharp with disapproval.

Mr Gray straightened his tie with a casual air. "I'll have the same as Lord Cavendish." He took a seat opposite the princess.

Aunt Beatrice cleared her throat, her expression tightening. "Mr Gray," she began, her voice cool but polite. "How good of you to finally join us. We were beginning to think you'd lost your way." Her eyes narrowed slightly, a silent display of her irritation.

"My apologies for the delay, Lady Hawthorne. An unforeseen business problem – fortunately, it was easily rectified with a bit of creative thinking." His tone was smooth as he glanced at the princess before turning his attention back to Aunt Beatrice.

The waiter returned with a tray of drinks, placing each one on the table. Alexander wasted no time, taking a large sip of his whisky and almost immediately ordering another. Elizabeth watched him, her concern deepening with each swift gulp.

As she turned her attention to Mr Gray, curiosity gnawed at her. How had he known the princess's drink preference? The Champs-Élysées with a twist of Meyer lemon was hardly a common choice. Neither Princess Sofia nor Mr Gray had mentioned a past acquaintance, yet the familiarity in the way he had ordered for her suggested otherwise.

Elizabeth couldn't ignore the subtle change in Sofia since Mr Gray's arrival. The princess, who had been lively and animated, now seemed more subdued. Her earlier enthusiasm dimmed. In contrast, Mr Gray maintained his usual conviviality, his charm undiminished by the shift in atmosphere.

What puzzled Elizabeth even more were the looks passing between Sofia and Mr Gray. There was an unspoken understanding in those glances, something just beneath the surface, adding to the growing list of questions swirling in her mind about the princess.

The lights dimmed, signalling the start of the performance. Guests hurried to their feet, leaving half-finished drinks behind. Princess Sofia, however, tipped her head back and drained her glass. Aunt Beatrice's eyes widened.

As people settled into their seats, Sofia leaned towards Alexander, her voice low. His brow creased briefly before he nodded and stood. Sofia slid into the vacated chair next to Aunt Beatrice.

"The person in front of me is dreadfully tall," Sofia sighed, shifting in the chair. "I can't see a thing from my seat."

Elizabeth glanced at the row in front, where a man of average height was settling into his seat. Odd that the princess would claim he was blocking her view. She caught Alexander's eye as he took the vacated chair, and he offered her a small, weary smile.

Why would the princess avoid sitting next to Mr Gray? The two seemed to share some sort of history, one that obviously carried a degree of tension between them.

Elizabeth pushed her questions aside as the orchestra struck the first few notes. The curtain lifted, revealing *Titta Ruffo*, the acclaimed Italian baritone. His powerful voice surged through the auditorium, captivating the audience with his rendition of "Largo al factotum" from *The Barber of Seville*.

Elizabeth found herself swept away by *Ruffo's* sheer energy and dynamism. Every note he sang resonated with a palpable passion, his charismatic stage presence commanding attention. When he concluded with a dramatic flourish, the audience erupted into thunderous applause, the sound echoing through the ornate space.

The applause had barely subsided when *Rosa Ponselle* took the stage, her commanding presence instantly captivating the crowd. She launched into "Casta Diva" from *Bellini's Norma*, her voice a spellbinding blend of power and delicacy that sent shivers down Elizabeth's spine. The audience held their breath, entranced by the haunting beauty of her performance.

Beniamino Gigli followed, his rich tenor filling the auditorium with a heart-wrenching rendition of "E lucevan le stelle" from *Puccini's Tosca*. His emotive delivery and flawless technique drew tears from more than a few eyes, including Elizabeth's. She glanced at Meli, who sat mesmerised, her hands clasped tightly in her lap.

As the first half of the performance drew to a close, the trio of singers returned to the stage for a powerful ensemble piece, "Libiamo ne' lieti calici" from *Verdi's La Traviata*. Their voices melded in perfect harmony, bringing the first act to a rousing, celebratory conclusion. The audience erupted into enthusiastic applause, the sound filling the grand auditorium.

Elizabeth's gaze swept the auditorium, but neither Alexander nor the princess were in their seats. Leaning in towards Meli, she murmured, "I'm worried about Alexander. He's been acting strangely all evening. I'm going to step out and see if I can find where he's disappeared to."

She slipped away, into the crowded foyer. A flash of golden hair caught her eye, and she spotted the princess and Alexander in a secluded alcove.

From a distance, she noticed the princess's body language was agitated, her gestures sharp and pointed as she spoke. In contrast, his posture was slumped, his expression strained as he listened.

The princess spun on her heel, her silk gown swishing as she stormed off. Nearby patrons quickly averted their eyes. Alexander stood motionless for a moment, then trudged to the bar. "Whisky, neat," he muttered, his shoulders sagging.

Elizabeth wove through the crowd, coming to a stop beside Alexander. "Where's the princess?"

Alexander's fingers tightened around his glass. He glanced over Elizabeth's shoulder before meeting her gaze. "She's mingling with some acquaintances." The corner of his mouth twitched upward. "I seized the opportunity for a quiet drink."

Elizabeth's hand hovered near his arm, her eyes searching his face.

Alexander's knuckles whitened around his glass. He stared into the amber liquid, his eyes unfocused. "A man has his limits, Elizabeth," he murmured, his voice barely audible above the crowd's chatter. "I can't—" He swallowed hard. "It has to end. Tonight."

A chill ran through Elizabeth. Before she could respond, a voice cut in from behind her.

"Sounds serious."

Elizabeth startled. Neither of them had heard Mr Gray approach.

Alexander threw back his drink in one swift motion before slamming the empty glass onto the bar with a force that made it rattle. He swayed as he turned, almost stumbling into a nearby table. His steps zigzagged as he collided with several people, muttering slurred apologies as he went.

Mr Gray's gaze followed Alexander's unsteady retreat, his eyes glinting with calculation. "Looks like someone's got women troubles?"

Elizabeth stiffened, biting back a retort. "What makes you say that, Mr Gray?"

He leaned in, his voice low and conspiratorial. "Trust me, Lady Elizabeth, when a man gets himself all worked up like that, there's usually a woman at the root of it." A smirk played at the corners of his mouth.

Before Elizabeth could respond, the lights flickered, signalling the second half was about to begin. Relieved to escape Mr Gray and his opinions on women, before she said something she'd regret, she hurried back to her seat.

The lights dimmed, and *Ruffo's* powerful baritone exploded through the auditorium, his rendition of "Cortigiani, vil razza dannata" from *Rigoletto* holding the audience in its thrall. The music swelled, its intensity washing over Elizabeth in waves, sweeping her away to another realm. She clung to her seat, transfixed, until the final notes faded and the crowd erupted into a thunderous ovation.

Darkness descended once more, and Elizabeth's breath hitched as Ganna Walska glided onto the stage, a vision in crimson. The opening bars of *Puccini's* "Un bel dì, vedremo" swelled, and Ganna's voice took flight, each note searing the aria with haunting beauty that sent shivers racing down Elizabeth's spine.

As the last note died away, the audience surged to their feet, rapturous applause crashing through the theatre like a tidal wave. Overwhelming admiration flooded Elizabeth's heart, her friend's extraordinary talent leaving her awestruck.

Ganna's gaze swept across the auditorium, locking with Elizabeth's for a searing moment as she launched into the opening bars of "Sempre libera" from *Verdi's La Traviata*, her voice a mesmerising tapestry of power and grace.

The sheer magnificence of Ganna's performance held Elizabeth spellbound, the music weaving around her, through her, until she was lost in its embrace. She sat transfixed, scarcely daring to breathe until the last notes faded and the audience erupted, their thunderous applause almost shaking the very foundations of the Théâtre du Boulevard.

The final notes of Ganna's spellbinding performance lingered in the air as the audience stirred. Aunt Beatrice's lips pursed, a slight furrow forming between her brows as her gaze swept the crowd. "Where's Alexander?"

Princess Sofia's head tilted. "He mentioned stepping outside for a cigarette earlier."

Elizabeth's frown deepened. Odd – Alexander didn't smoke. The situation with the princess was weighing heavily on him. Squaring her shoulders, Elizabeth gave Aunt Beatrice a reassuring nod. "I'll look for him. I'm in need of a breath of fresh air myself."

Aunt Beatrice nodded absently, her attention already drawn back to the princess.

Weaving through the dispersing crowd, Elizabeth's gaze landed on the cocktail bar. There, amid the elegant surroundings, she spotted Alexander. He hunched over the polished counter, elbows propped on its surface, a glass of whisky cradled in his hands.

Catching sight of her in the mirror, Alexander's shoulders tensed. He raised his glass in a rueful gesture, amber liquid sloshing over the rim.

Elizabeth answered with a small, sympathetic smile, her heart aching at the turmoil etched across his features. Alexander faced the ultimate dichotomy – bear the shame and scandal of financial ruin or spend his life trapped in a loveless marriage necessitated by duty and familial expectations.

Chapter Seven

A SCREAM PIERCED THE early morning silence, echoing through Le Majestique's corridors. Elizabeth jolted awake, heart pounding. She sprang from the bed, grabbing her robe in one motion.

Adrenaline surged, shaking off sleep. She glanced at Meli's bed, ensuring her cousin was safe. Meli slept on, unaware of the commotion. Relieved, Elizabeth dashed across the sitting room, the plush carpet muffling her footsteps, and pushed open the door to the master bedroom.

Aunt Beatrice bolted upright, clutching her chest. Her eyes darted around the room, wild with confusion. "What on earth was that noise?"

Her voice shook. "And at this ungodly hour. It's barely six o'clock!"

Elizabeth tightened her robe. "I'm not sure, Aunt. Are you all right?"

"Yes, yes, I'm fine." She waved away Elizabeth's concern. "Although I can think of more pleasant ways to be woken."

Evelyn, already up, stood in the doorway, her expression tense. Elizabeth scanned her face for signs of distress. "What about you, Evelyn?"

Evelyn nodded. "I'm fine, Lady Elizabeth. Just a bit shaken."

Elizabeth's worry eased slightly. She turned and found Meli behind her, rubbing sleep from her eyes. "I'm going to see what's going on. Stay here with Aunt Beatrice and Evelyn, and lock the door after me," she instructed, placing a reassuring hand on Meli's shoulder.

Meli's eyes flared with frustration. "Why can't I come with you? I'm not a child, Elizabeth."

Elizabeth shook her head. "Please, Meli, do as I ask and stay here." Without waiting for a reply, she stepped into the corridor. Furtive glances met her from doors left ajar, guests peering out at the commotion. Worry gnawed at her;

the scream had sounded so desperate. What if someone had been hurt? She forced herself to stay calm, each step heavy with apprehension.

Further along, Paulette, one of the young maids, rushed out of a room, her face pale and eyes wide with terror. Elizabeth hurried towards her, concern etched on her features. She gripped Paulette's shoulders. "What's wrong?"

Paulette pointed inside the room, her hand trembling. "C'est terrible!" Tears streamed down her cheeks.

Elizabeth scanned the corridor for someone to take care of Paulette. She turned to find Meli right behind her, breathless. About to chastise her, Elizabeth stopped, realising she was glad Meli hadn't listened. "What about Aunt Beatrice and Evelyn?"

Meli held up the door key, eyes flashing with defiance. "I locked them inside."

Steeling herself, Elizabeth stepped into the suite, a pall of dread descending over her. Shattered glass and overturned furniture bore witness to a violent struggle, while the unmistakable scent of spilled perfume and the metallic tang of blood assaulted her senses.

Her eyes darted around the room, coming to rest on the motionless form of Princess Sofia. The once-dazzling champagne silk of her gown now resembled a deathly shroud. A pool of dried blood darkened the intricate patterns of the Persian rug beneath her, a grim testament to the violence that had claimed her life.

A chill ran down Elizabeth's spine as she knelt beside the princess. Up close, Sofia's skin appeared deathly pale, lacking the usual flush of life, and her once sparkling eyes staring vacantly at the ceiling above, forever frozen in a moment of unspeakable horror. Elizabeth's heart raced as she pressed trembling fingers to the princess's neck, praying for a faint pulse, a glimmer of hope – but the icy, unresponsive flesh beneath her touch confirmed her worst fears.

The sound of hurried footsteps drew Elizabeth's attention to the doorway, where Monsieur Róbert , the assistant manager, forced his way through the guests crowding the entrance. His gasp rang out as he took in the gruesome scene. "Is she...?" The question hung in the air, unfinished.

Elizabeth's nod was almost imperceptible as the grim reality settled in with a sickening weight.

She rose to her feet, her composure steadying as urgency hardened her voice. "Monsieur Robert, we must get everyone out and notify the authorities immediately." Her tone brooked no argument, her eyes conveying the gravity of the situation.

The guests lingered, necks craning and eyes wide as they inched backwards. With each step, they stole glances over their shoulders, desperate for one last look at the grisly scene. Hushed whispers rippled through the crowd like a rolling wave as they made their way back to their rooms.

"How dreadful! Who could have done such a thing?" a woman murmured, her voice tinged with shock.

"A murder right here in Le Majestique! Whatever next?" a man exclaimed, shaking his head in disbelief.

"Do you think it was a robbery?" another guest speculated. "There were several pieces of the princess's jewellery that I was quite envious of."

With the guests dispersed and Monsieur Róbert gone to notify the authorities, Elizabeth turned her attention back to the trembling Paulette. "Meli, please escort Paulette downstairs. Ask the housekeeper to provide her with a brandy or a cup of sweet tea – it will help to calm her."

Meli nodded, concern etched on her face. She wrapped an arm around Paulette's quivering shoulders, guiding the distraught maid towards the stairs. "Come on, let's get you something to help settle your nerves."

Elizabeth watched them leave, bracing herself before reentering the princess's suite. As she stepped over the threshold, her gaze swept across the scene, the chaos and disarray bearing silent witness to the violent struggle that had taken place.

Her eyes scanned the room, her mind racing as she examined the evidence, determined to gather any information that might aid the police. Elizabeth circled the room, her steps light to avoid disturbing the potential evidence. A smear of blood on the edge of the bedside table drew her eye. Leaning in, she scrutinised the crimson stain, considering if the princess had stumbled and struck her head there. Elizabeth's brow furrowed at the thought.

Turning to the princess, Elizabeth knelt beside the lifeless form, her fingers parting the golden locks now matted with dried blood. A deep, jagged gash on the woman's temple came into view, the severity of the wound and the pooled blood suggesting a heavy blow. Elizabeth's gaze swept the room, searching for a potential weapon.

The overturned furniture and scattered belongings painted a picture of chaos, but to Elizabeth's surprise, apart from a few ornaments, nothing appeared damaged or broken. It almost seemed as if someone had orchestrated the disarray. Elizabeth's fingers drummed against her leg as she struggled to piece together the puzzle.

Then her eyes landed on the princess's jewellery box abandoned on the floor. If this had been a robbery, why would the thief have left behind the exquisite silver box inlaid with onyx, not to mention the diamond bracelet the princess was wearing? Elizabeth's frown deepened.

Something wasn't right.

Hurried footsteps echoed through the corridor as Monsieur Róbert returned with the police. Chief Inspector Gérard Dubois led the way, his weathered face set in a stern expression. Detective Maxime Detective Lefèvre followed closely, his intense blue eyes scanning the room as he scribbled notes on a small notepad.

Elizabeth felt a wave of relief at the sight of the police. Finally, she could share her observations and insights. She straightened her posture, eager to assist the investigation.

Chief Inspector Dubois's eyes narrowed as he entered the room, taking in the chaotic scene. He fixed Elizabeth with a steely gaze. "Chief Inspector Dubois." His booming voice sliced through the tense silence. "Who are you, and what are you doing in here? This is a crime scene; you have no business being here."

Elizabeth met his gaze with defiance. "I'm Elizabeth—" She paused, catching his dismissive expression, then corrected herself. "Lady Elizabeth Hawthorne. I was one of the first to find Princess Sofia. I've been making observations that might help—"

Chief Inspector Dubois raised a hand, cutting her off. "Observations? This is not a game." His tone was sharp. "Now, if you wouldn't mind running along, Lady Hawthorne, some of us have a job to do."

Elizabeth opened her mouth to protest, but Chief Inspector Dubois dismissed her with a wave. He turned to Detective Lefèvre, who continued his note-taking. "Secure the area, and make sure no one else disturbs the evidence."

Frustration bubbled inside Elizabeth, but she refused to be deterred. Clenching her fists, she stepped forward, determined to share her findings. "Chief Inspector, there are details here that suggest—"

The chief inspector glared at her, his patience waning. "Mademoiselle, if you have any relevant information, then by all means give it to Detective Lefèvre … on your way out."

Meli burst through the door, her dark curls in disarray and a flush of exertion on her cheeks. She leaned against the doorframe, breathless.

"Elizabeth, I'm so sorry I've been gone for so long. The staff were all in such an uproar downstairs over the news of Princess Sofia's death. I got caught up in the commotion." She paused, noticing the two police officers. Her gaze flickered between them, a hint of self-consciousness creeping into her expression.

Chief Inspector Dubois fixed Meli with a stern glare, his mouth twisting into a disapproving frown. He muttered under his breath, "More hysterical women, just what I need."

Meli turned to face him, cheeks flushed with anger. She straightened her posture and squared her shoulders. "Hysterical? I beg your pardon, monsieur, but I am hardly hysterical." Her tone was sharp.

Detective Lefèvre stepped forward, a slow smile curving his lips. "*Bonjour, mademoiselle.* I'm Detective Maxime Detective Lefèvre." He held Meli's gaze a heartbeat longer than was proper.

Meli's cheeks flushed as she returned the detective's gaze. "It's a pleasure to meet you, Detective Lefèvre." The corners of her lips turned up in a shy smile.

Chief Inspector Dubois let out a derisive snort. "Enough of this nonsense. We have a murder to investigate, and we don't have time for the fancies of two excitable young ladies." He turned to Elizabeth and Meli, his expression unyielding. "I must insist that you both leave the premises immediately."

Elizabeth's jaw tightened, and she gave a curt nod. "Very well, Chief Inspector." She placed a firm hand on Meli's elbow, steering her towards the door. "Come, Meli, we don't want to waste any more of the Chief Inspector's precious time."

Meli followed, casting one last glance at Detective Lefèvre, who held her gaze with a subtle, appreciative smile. They walked down the corridor in tense silence, the weight of the morning's events hanging between them.

Reaching their suite, Meli broke the silence, her voice laced with concern. "Are you really going to leave the investigation to Chief Inspector Dubois?" She hesitated, scepticism clear in her eyes. "He seems a little..." she trailed off, searching for the right words.

Elizabeth paused, her hand hovering over the brass doorknob. She let out a measured breath, her brow furrowing with frustration. "Pompous? Overbearing?" She shook her head. "Something tells me Chief Inspector Dubois couldn't find honey in a beehive, let alone solve a murder."

Chapter Eight

Silence smothered Le Jardin Matin, snuffing out the usual chatter and vibrant ambience like candles in a draft. Elizabeth swept her gaze across a sea of drawn faces and mournful sighs.

Beside Elizabeth, Meli fidgeted with her napkin, her usual vibrance dimmed to a muted flicker. Her toffee-coloured eyes darted about the table, her brow creased with a weighted uncertainty at odds with her usual carefree spirit.

Elizabeth spared a glance, giving Meli's hand a gentle squeeze. Her cousin returned a wavering smile, but worry lingered in her gaze.

Across from them, Aunt Beatrice pressed her lips into a rigid line, her fingers drumming an agitated beat against the crisp linen. Displeasure radiated from the matriarch's ramrod posture as her discerning gaze swept the room, cataloguing every detail.

Beside Aunt Beatrice, Evelyn sat in weighted silence, her eyes fixed on the untouched plate before her. Elizabeth caught the subtle tightening of the other woman's jaw, a rare breach in Evelyn's composure that betrayed the turmoil lurking beneath the surface.

"A murder! At Le Majestique. I simply can't believe it," Aunt Beatrice huffed, a breath of disbelief escaping her lips. "I blame the management." Her mouth twisted with distaste as her gaze returned to the breakfast spread, nostrils flaring with disapproval.

Elizabeth reached out, laying a gentle hand on her aunt's arm. "Aunt Beatrice, I don't think we can blame Monsieur Marchand—" She faltered, doubt flickering across her features as that nagging unease refused to subside.

Aunt Beatrice's eyes narrowed to slits, a stubborn resolve hardening her expression as she dismissed Elizabeth's words with a brusque wave of her hand. "Gaston would never have allowed this to happen." She squared her shoulders, her voice sharp. "The world's changing, Elizabeth, and not for the better."

Meli tilted her head, her voice dipping to a discreet murmur. "Do you think one of the other guests could be the murderer?" Her eyes swept the room, narrowed with suspicion.

Aunt Beatrice's head snapped around, her brow furrowing at Meli's words. "Nonsense, child. Le Majestique is a most respectable establishment, or at least it was, under Monsieur Gáston's steady hand. But nevertheless, I'm certain the police will soon find whoever it was who carried out such a heinous act."

Elizabeth caught Meli's eye, and the two exchanged a weighted glance, their faith in the self-important Chief Inspector Dubois far more limited than Aunt Beatrice's confidence. Elizabeth couldn't help but recall their previous encounter, the way he'd dismissed her observations with such condescending arrogance, preferring to leave the important work to the men he deemed more capable.

A sense of unease settled over her as she turned her attention back to the room.

The breakfast room, typically abuzz with chatter, now felt stifled. Conversations were hushed, and weary gazes flickered about, as if everyone shared the same gnawing fear. Was the murderer among them, hiding in plain sight?

The door to Le Jardin Matin swung open, drawing every eye as Alexander entered, his dishevelled appearance causing a ripple of concern to spread through the room. His chestnut hair, usually neatly styled, now fell in unkempt disarray across his brow. His clothes, rumpled and wrinkled, spoke of a restless night. His face, pale and drawn, only emphasised the redness rimming his eyes and the unshaven stubble along his jaw.

Aunt Beatrice's restless fingers stilled on the table. Her eyes narrowed as she took in Alexander's distressed state. "Poor man." She shook her head. "He must be devastated."

Elizabeth's heart sank as she watched Alexander stumble, his usual confident stride replaced by a weary shuffle as he made his way to their table and collapsed into a chair with a heavy sigh. He raised a trembling hand to rub at his temples, as if the simple action pained him.

Leaning forward, Aunt Beatrice's brow creased with worry. "Alexander, you look dreadful. How are you bearing up?"

Alexander winced as he shook his head. "I … didn't sleep well. Feeling a bit off," he managed, his voice strained and unsteady.

Nodding sympathetically, Aunt Beatrice reached out to give his hand a reassuring pat. "It's no wonder, after what's happened."

Elizabeth studied Alexander, her worry deepening as her gaze narrowed. She leaned forward. "Alexander, what time did you and the princess arrive back at the hotel?"

A frown flickered across Alexander's features as he struggled to recall, his eyes darting away from Elizabeth's piercing stare. "I'm … er, I'm not sure," he admitted, the uncertainty in his tone palpable.

Aunt Beatrice tsked, her hand still resting atop his as she soothed, "It's been such a dreadful shock, no wonder you can't think straight."

Elizabeth's eyes widened, realisation dawning on her features. "Alexander," she murmured, her voice laced with a newfound gentleness, "you don't know, do you?"

"Know what?" Alexander's hand trembled as he lifted the black coffee to his lips, the cup rattling against the saucer.

"Princess Sofia was found dead this morning." Elizabeth's words hung in the air, heavy with the weight of their implication.

The cup slipped from Alexander's grasp, the scalding liquid splashing across his thigh. He leapt to his feet, sending the chair toppling backwards with a resounding crash. All eyes in the breakfast room snapped towards their table. Aunt Beatrice's throat bobbed. Her eyes darted from face to face, meeting the curious stares of the other guests before darting away.

"Dead ... how do you mean dead?" Alexander brushed at the front of his trousers with a napkin, oblivious to the waiters, who rushed to clear the mess. "Did she have an accident?"

Elizabeth shook her head, her gaze never wavering from Alexander's pallid face. "I'm so sorry to have to tell you this, Alexander, but the princess ... was murdered."

At her words, Alexander's complexion drained of colour, his features etched with a haunting vulnerability as he slumped back into his chair. His gaze swept across the room, briefly fixating on Clara Hicks, an odd, unreadable expression passing between them.

Elizabeth caught Meli's eye. Her cousin's tight-lipped expression echoed her own misgivings. Alexander's evasiveness troubled her. It was rare for him to be anything other than forthright. Yet, despite this uncharacteristic behaviour, she remained certain of one thing – he was no murderer.

All conversation in the breakfast room ground to a halt as Chief Inspector Dubois, accompanied by Detective Lefèvre, swept through the double doors, their air of self-importance commanding the attention of every diner. Elizabeth watched, pulse quickening, as he paused in the centre of the room, his sharp gaze sweeping across the gathered guests, scrutinising them like a hawk eyeing its prey.

The detective raised his hand. A waiter rushed over, pointing shakily towards Elizabeth's table. The man's gaze fixed on Alexander, his eyes hard. "Mister Cavendish," he called, his voice silencing the room's whispers.

Beside Elizabeth, Aunt Beatrice stiffened, her lips pressing into a thin, disapproving line. Elizabeth caught the subtle tightening of the older woman's jaw, a rare breach in her composure that betrayed her discomfort at Chief Inspector Dubois's public spectacle. "It's Lord Cavendish," Aunt Beatrice retorted, her tone laced with polite but pointed irritation. "And you are?"

The inspector flicked a dismissive glance at Aunt Beatrice. "Chief Inspector Dubois." He continued without missing a beat. "I understand you were the last person seen with Princess Sofia de' Medici last night, Lord Cavendish."

Alexander flinched under Elizabeth's touch. "Was … was I?" he stammered, his voice wavering.

The chief inspector's jaw tightened with frustration. "Where were you between midnight and four o'clock this morning?"

Alexander's hesitation was palpable. His gaze darted to Aunt Beatrice and then to the floor. "I … I can't remember exactly. I think I was … I must have been…" His voice trailed off, uncertainty thickening his words.

Elizabeth's heart pounded, each beat a drum of rising dread. Beads of sweat formed on Alexander's brow, his hands trembling as they gripped the table. Out of the corner of her eye, she caught Clara Hicks casting quick, nervous glances toward Alexander.

Chief Inspector Dubois's patience frayed, his voice slicing through the tense silence. "Were you with Princess Sofia the entire night?"

Aunt Beatrice's eyes flashed with indignation, her cheeks reddening. "Really, Chief Inspector."

Alexander's eyes flicked to Clara again, a fleeting look passing between them. He swallowed hard, his words catching in his throat. "I … I'd rather not say."

He leaned closer, his tone sharp. "This is a murder investigation. It's not the time to be coy. I'll ask again. Where were you between midnight and four o'clock this morning?"

The silence stretched, thick with tension.

Aunt Beatrice's eyes blazed. She leaned forward. "Chief Inspector Dubois, can't you see he's in shock? Surely this can wait."

His gaze swept over Aunt Beatrice, his nostrils flaring. "Murder waits for no one, Lady Hawthorne. Not even for Lord Cavendish."

Aunt Beatrice's face flushed with anger. She drew herself up, her eyes narrowing with indignation. "This is most unacceptable. I shall be speaking to your superiors."

Dubois's frustration deepened, the hard line of his mouth set. "Where were you between—"

Alexander's eyes darted around the room, landing momentarily on Clara Hicks again. "Alone ... I was alone. If you must know."

Elizabeth's gaze sharpened, noting the subtle exchanges between Alexander and Clara. Something felt off, like a piece of the puzzle was missing. Her gut churned, sensing that Alexander was holding something back.

His jaw clenched. "Very well. In that case, you leave me no choice. Detective, the cuffs."

Elizabeth's breath caught in her throat as Detective Lefèvre stepped forward, producing a pair of handcuffs. Meli's eyes widened, the spark from their previous meeting replaced by a sharp, reproachful glare. "No! You can't do this!"

He fixed her with a stony stare. "I'm afraid I must. Lord Cavendish, you're under arrest on suspicion of the murder of Princess Sofia de' Medici."

Gasps and whispers erupted around the breakfast room. Elizabeth's eyes flitted across the room, seeing the wide eyes and hushed exchanges. Anger flared at Chief Inspector Dubois's callousness, his blatant disregard for the humiliation Alexander was enduring.

Detective Lefèvre clicked the cuffs around Alexander's wrists, the sound a harsh punctuation to the chief inspector's declaration. Alexander's face went pale, desperation etched on his face.

Aunt Beatrice's fingers tightened around her clutch, her knuckles stark against the fabric. "This is an outrage," she bit out through gritted teeth.

Elizabeth placed a calming hand on her aunt's arm, offering some measure of comfort even as her own fear threatened to overwhelm her. She caught Meli's eye, her cousin's toffee eyes wide with shock. The sense of dread gnawed at her insides, twisting her stomach into knots.

As Detective Lefèvre and Chief Inspector Dubois led Alexander away, Elizabeth's eyes followed them, a knot of anxiety tightening in her chest.

Alexander was no murderer. Elizabeth knew this as surely as she knew her own name. But his evasiveness gnawed at her. What was he hiding? And would uncovering his secret prove his innocence – or seal his fate?

Chapter Nine

GASPS SPREAD LIKE WILDFIRE through Le Jardin Matin as Chief Inspector Dubois led Alexander away in handcuffs. The breakfast room, typically buzzing with animated conversation, now hummed with shocked whispers and rustling newspapers. His public spectacle was both calculated and gratuitous.

Aunt Beatrice's face briefly betrayed her shock, but she quickly regained her composure, rising from her seat with unshakable poise. Back straight and chin high, she led the way out of the breakfast room, ignoring the stares and whispers.

Tension filled the air during their return to the suite. Aunt Beatrice opted for the lift, forsaking her usual aversion to the modern contraption in her haste to escape the crowd's scrutiny. She stood tall, her gaze fixed ahead, ignoring the other guests' stares. Once in the suite, her composure shattered. She strode across the room, her hands twisting together.

"This is a disaster." Aunt Beatrice's voice was low but sharp. "If word of Alexander's arrest reaches England, it will ruin him. And we," she paused, straightening her back. "We'll be tainted by association."

Elizabeth stepped closer. "Aunt Beatrice, we don't know all the facts yet."

Aunt Beatrice turned away, resuming her pacing. "Facts? The fact is, this scandal could destroy us all."

Evelyn appeared with a glass of water. "Perhaps you should sit for a moment, Lady Hawthorne."

"Sit?" Aunt Beatrice's eyes flashed. She waved Evelyn away. "How can I sit while our good name is at stake, Evelyn?"

Elizabeth met Evelyn's worried gaze, then squared her shoulders. "I'm going to the police station. I'll speak with the chief inspector and find out what evidence he claims to have against Alexander. I'm sure we'll have this whole thing cleared up by lunchtime." She forced a reassuring smile for her aunt's benefit.

As Aunt Beatrice resumed her agitated pacing, Elizabeth caught Meli's eye and discreetly gestured towards the door. Meli nodded, following her cousin into the corridor.

Elizabeth drew Meli aside, her voice low. "Watch over Aunt Beatrice, will you? I fear this ordeal might take its toll. She's not as ... resilient as she once was."

"Don't worry, I'll tend to things here." Meli squeezed her hand. "Good luck with the chief inspector."

Elizabeth's confident words rang hollow in her own ears as she made her way to the lift. She had little faith in Chief Inspector Dubois's investigative skills, and Alexander's secrecy troubled her. But for now, offering her aunt a glimmer of hope, however fleeting, would have to suffice.

The lift doors opened, and Elizabeth stepped out into the foyer. Curious stares and hushed murmurs greeted her, the morning's events clearly fodder for gossip. Elizabeth lifted her chin, her face a mask of calm determination as she strode across the room. At the entrance, she caught the doorman's eye, and he summoned a taxi with a sharp whistle.

Seated in the back of a motorcar winding through the bustling streets of Cannes, Elizabeth's mind raced. She knew Alexander was no murderer. So why wouldn't he disclose his whereabouts to the chief inspector? What could he possibly be hiding?

The lively streets outside the taxi window seemed to mock her. Cafés bustled with morning rituals, their laughter and conversations a cruel contrast to the turmoil churning inside her.

The taxi slowed as it approached the police station, a grandiose structure with a neoclassical design. Its imposing grey stone façade and tall arched windows gave it an air of unyielding authority. The bold, black letters of Gendarmerie Nationale above the entrance served as a stark reminder of the power held within.

Stepping out of the motorcar, Elizabeth took a moment to steady herself. The station buzzed with activity, officers moving briskly in and out, their serious expressions reflecting the gravity of her mission. Taking a deep breath, she pushed open the heavy wooden door.

Inside, desks formed an erratic maze, each one piled high with paperwork. The muted murmurs of conversation mixed with the occasional clack of typewriter keys created a constant hum of activity. Officers darted around, their uniforms a blur of navy blue and brass buttons.

Elizabeth made her way to the front desk. "*Bonjour*." She offered the officer a warm smile, her eyes steady. "I'd like to speak to Chief Inspector Dubois about Lord Cavendish."

The officer at the desk barely glanced up. "*Attendez ici*." Without another word, he disappeared through a door at the back of the room.

The police station felt cold and unwelcoming, its stark, grey walls lined with rows of filing cabinets and notice boards cluttered with wanted posters and official notices. Fluorescent lights cast a harsh glare over the scene, illuminating the worn wooden floorboards. Elizabeth caught the occasional curious glance from the officers, their serious expressions underscoring the gravity of the situation.

The door burst open, and Chief Inspector Dubois strode out, the officer trailing behind. His eyes locked onto Elizabeth, a flicker of irritation crossing his features.

Elizabeth held his gaze, her chin held high. "I'd like to speak to Lord Cavendish, if you would be so kind."

His lips twisted into a sneer. "Speak to him?" He let out a snort. "Lord Cavendish has been charged with murder. This is not a café for socialising, Mademoiselle." He chuckled, a harsh sound echoing off the sterile walls.

Detective Lefèvre glanced up from his papers, observing the exchange with a keen eye.

Elizabeth's voice remained firm. "If you won't let me speak to him, then I'd like to know what evidence you have against him."

His smile faded, replaced by a look of incredulity. "This is a murder investigation. I'm not divulging that information with you." He gestured dismissively toward the door. "Go back to your hotel and leave the police work to the real police." Turning on his heel, he marched back into his office, the door slamming shut with a definitive thud.

Detective Lefèvre made his way across the room with an air of nonchalance. Catching Elizabeth's eye, he gave a subtle jerk of his head, indicating she should follow. She scanned the room for prying eyes, then slipped through the side door after him.

Together, they navigated a maze of musty hallways, the walls covered with peeling paint and cracked plaster. Detective Lefèvre angled closer, his voice a hushed whisper. "Dubois is under a lot of pressure from the mayor to make a quick arrest." He glanced around before continuing, "He wants to reassure the elite that Cannes is safe, even if it means making an arrest without solid evidence."

Elizabeth's eyes flashed with outrage. "So he's prioritising financial gains over justice? But why arrest Alexander?"

"The princess and Lord Cavendish were seen arguing last night at the casino." Detective Lefèvre's expression tightened as he spoke.

"Who saw them?" Elizabeth's eyes narrowed.

Detective Lefèvre shook his head slightly. "I'm sorry, Lady Hawthorne, I've already said too much."

"Alexander is no murderer, Detective." Elizabeth's voice remained unwavering, her gaze steady.

Detective Lefèvre met her eyes, urgency in his expression. "Then you need to find the evidence to prove it."

As they reached the holding cells, he turned to Elizabeth, his eyes flickering with unease. "I can give you a few minutes, but no more." He stepped back, leaving Elizabeth and Alexander alone.

She peered through the bars on the metal door, taking in the dimly lit space. The cell was small and severe, with grey walls and a single narrow bench. A flickering light cast eerie shadows, adding to the oppressive atmosphere.

Elizabeth's heart clenched at the sight of Alexander, his handsome face etched with exhaustion. As he stood, he tried to project strength, but the starkness of the cell only amplified the surreal agony of seeing him like this.

"Elizabeth," Alexander's voice was a strained whisper as he stepped closer, his eyes searching hers. "What are you doing here?" He gripped the bars, knuckles white.

Elizabeth took a deep breath, steadying herself. "I had to see you, Alexander, to make sure you're all right." Her voice was calm, hiding the storm within her. She clasped her hands to stop them from trembling.

He nodded, the corners of his mouth lifting briefly. "And Aunt Beatrice? How is she faring?" His hand moved to his temple, fingers pressing lightly against his skin.

"She's had a shock," Elizabeth admitted. "But Meli and Evelyn are with her." She noted the tension in his shoulders, the way his posture drooped under the weight of their predicament. "You know Aunt Beatrice, despite appearances, family always comes first."

Alexander's shoulders sagged, the pressure visible. He ran a hand through his dishevelled hair, a gesture Elizabeth knew well. "I hate to think of her so upset. This whole thing is a nightmare. I didn't do it, Elizabeth … I swear."

Elizabeth leaned closer. "But why won't you tell the police where you were at the time of the murder?"

Alexander looked away, his jaw tight. "I told you ... I can't remember. I got a little squiffy and..."

"Do you remember going to the casino?" Elizabeth pressed, eyes locked on his.

"Vaguely." He frowned, struggling to recall the hazy details.

"And the argument with the princess?" Elizabeth's gaze fixed on him.

"Argument...?" Confusion flickered in his eyes. "I don't recall any argument."

Detective Lefèvre's footsteps echoed, signalling the end of their meeting. He approached Elizabeth, a hint of nervousness in his eyes. "I'm sorry, Lady Hawthorne. It's time for you to leave."

Detective Lefèvre led Elizabeth through a dank corridor, his steps quick but measured. He paused at an unmarked door, casting a sideways glance at her. "And Mademoiselle Diomaros? How is she?" His tone was casual, but his eyes held a subtle spark of interest.

Elizabeth noticed the shift in his demeanour when he spoke about her cousin. "Meli is a lot more resilient than she looks." She watched as Detective Lefèvre's lips curved into a small smile, his eyes softening.

"Yes, she's very ... spirited." Warmth crept into his voice as he pushed open the door, gesturing for Elizabeth to step through.

Before she exited, Detective Lefèvre turned back to her. "If there's anything you need, Lady Hawthorne, please let me know."

Elizabeth offered a small, appreciative smile. "Thank you, Detective." She stepped out onto the bustling streets, the door closing behind her. The lively energy of Cannes enveloped her, banishing the chill of the police station.

Elizabeth quickened her pace. Chief Inspector Dubois had only circumstantial evidence against Alexander. There was still time to uncover the real murderer and clear his name, but she had to act swiftly. If news of the scandal reached England...

Elizabeth rounded the corner of the police station. A wall of suits and hats blocked her path – journalists, their notepads open and pencils poised. Chief Inspector Dubois stood before them, chest puffed out, his voice carrying across the gathered crowd. Elizabeth slowed her pace, tilting her head to catch his words.

He spread his arms, a triumphant gleam in his eyes and a slight smirk curling his lips. "*L'arrestation de Alexander Cavendish … le meurtre.*"

Elizabeth strained to catch the meaning. "Arrest … Alexander Cavendish … murder." The implications were clear, and a wave of dread washed over her at the thought of the scandal spreading further.

Her stomach churned with anxiety. This public announcement meant the story would soon be everywhere. If the French press had already got hold of it, the British newspapers would inevitably follow. The thought of Lord Alexander Cavendish's name splashed across headlines, associated with murder, was unbearable. The scandal would devastate not only Alexander, but also the entire family. Aunt Beatrice, in particular, would be horrified. Their reputation, upheld over generations, was at risk of being irreparably tarnished.

She quickened her pace. Time was against her. She had to find the evidence to clear Alexander's name, whatever it took.

Chapter Ten

ELIZABETH'S EYES SNAPPED OPEN, the remnants of sleep dissolving into the early morning light. Yesterday's chaos lingered in her mind, each moment replaying itself with relentless precision. Alexander's arrest loomed over her, a dark cloud that refused to lift. She had no doubt of his innocence, but proving it would be a challenge. Aunt Beatrice's constant worry and refusal to leave their suite only added to her anxiety.

Elizabeth eased out of bed, careful not to wake her slumbering cousin. She tiptoed to the wardrobe, selecting a pastel floral blouse and a flowing cream-coloured skirt. Behind the dressing screen, she changed swiftly. Emerging, she smoothed the skirt over her hips and buttoned the last pearl button at her collar. A quick brush tamed her raven bob. With a last glance at her sleeping cousin, she left the room and took the lift to reception.

The garden offered a much-needed respite from Elizabeth's swirling thoughts as she wandered the winding paths. Fragrant lavender beds and vibrant rose bushes flanked her way.

An image of Aunt Beatrice's anxious face flashed in her mind, the potential repercussions of Alexander's arrest weighing heavily on the matriarch. At least Aunt Beatrice remained blissfully unaware of Chief Inspector Dubois's inflammatory statement to the press – for now, anyway.

Elizabeth paused, drawing in a deep, calming breath. The intoxicating scents of jasmine and gardenias blending with the salty Mediterranean sea-breeze, infusing her with a sense of clarity.

She'd telephone Cybil Hughes, the sharp-witted journalist from *The Times* who had assisted with a delicate family matter months earlier. Cybil would know whether news of Alexander's arrest had reached the British papers yet.

Elizabeth swept back into the hotel, her steps swift as she made a beeline to the reception desk. Monsieur Marchand greeted her with a warm smile. "*Bonjour*, Lady Elizabeth. You're up and about early this morning?"

"I'm afraid a restless night drove me out." She returned a polite smile and let her gaze sweep the lobby. "But a stroll through your lovely gardens has done wonders to clear my mind."

Marchand's chest swelled with pride. He straightened, his eyes brightening as he watched her. "Our gardens are the envy of the Riviera. I trust you found the fresh air and greenery restorative?"

Elizabeth gave a slight nod. "Indeed, Monsieur Marchand. They provided a welcome respite."

"And how fares Lady Hawthorne? We haven't had the pleasure of her company since … I do hope she is well?" Marchand's expression held a hint of genuine concern.

Elizabeth's reply was gentle yet firm, betraying the faint unease that lingered beneath the surface. "She's well, Monsieur, if a little low in spirits at present."

He nodded, his brow furrowing with empathy. "And Lord Cavendish... Please accept my most sincere apologies for the public spectacle. The Chief Inspector's behaviour was most intolerable."

Elizabeth arched a brow, her lips tightening into a disapproving line. "I daresay the chief inspector was far more concerned with appearances than conducting a proper investigation."

Marchand looked momentarily taken aback. "*Pardon?*"

Elizabeth flicked her wrist in a dismissive gesture. "No matter. Monsieur Marchand, I find myself in need of a small favour, if you would be so kind."

Monsieur Marchand straightened, his attention locked on her. "Of course, anything at all, Lady Elizabeth."

"I require the use of your private telephone for a most important call to London," she explained, her voice steady despite the faint drumming of her fingers against the counter. "It's a rather delicate matter that demands discretion."

He inclined his head respectfully. "I shall see to it personally," he assured her.

Before Elizabeth could say more, a sudden commotion in the foyer caught Marchand's attention. He turned, his eyes narrowing as he spotted a middle-aged guest, face flushed with anger, confronting Monsieur Robert, the assistant manager. The man's hands fisted at his sides, his stance aggressive as he leaned in. "This is unacceptable! My wife's jewellery is missing, and I demand action!"

"Excuse me a moment, Lady Elizabeth." Monsieur Marchand covered the space in a few quick strides. Holding up his palms in a placating gesture, he turned to the agitated guest, his voice taking on a soothing, diplomatic tone. "Monsieur, please. What seems to be the problem?"

He turned to Monsieur Robert, his voice dropping to a low, measured tone. Elizabeth observed the exchange, her curiosity rising. When Marchand's gaze flicked towards her, she feigned interest in a vase of fragrant flowers on the counter.

The recollection of Madame Dupont's distraught pleas about a missing necklace just a few days prior resurfaced in Elizabeth's thoughts. An uneasy furrow formed between her brows as she considered the implications – could it be that a jewel thief was indeed targeting the guests at Le Majestique?

"Let's continue this discussion in my office," Monsieur Marchand suggested, attempting to steer the guest away from the public eye.

The agitated guest hesitated for a moment, then gave a curt nod. "Very well."

Marchand gestured for him to follow as they made their way towards the private office, disappearing behind the closed door. Elizabeth remained nearby, pretending to examine a potted plant on a nearby table as she strained to overhear the conversation.

Muffled voices sounded from within the office, the guest's tone still laced with anger. "There's nothing to discuss. My wife's earrings have been stolen. I insist you call the police immediately."

Marchand's response was more measured, though Elizabeth could detect a hint of frustration. "Monsieur, I assure you our deposit boxes are extremely secure. There must be some mistake."

"Then the thief must be one of your staff," the guest retorted, the accusation clear even through the closed door.

"Monsieur, I can promise you our staff are entirely trustworthy," Monsieur Marchand countered quickly. "This is just a misunderstanding."

The guest let out an exasperated sigh. "Very well, but I'm warning you, Marchand, if you don't find them—"

Monsieur Marchand stepped forward, his voice steady. "I give you my personal assurance this matter will be resolved. You have my word as manager of Le Majestique."

Sensing the conversation nearing its end, Elizabeth scurried away from the office door, hurrying to reclaim her spot by the reception desk. She'd scarcely settled herself when the door flew open, the agitated guest storming out, his face still flushed with anger. His heavy strides betraying his lingering frustration.

Marchand emerged next, his normally composed façade slightly ruffled. He paused, his gaze lingering on the departing guest for a moment before turning towards Elizabeth.

She met his gaze, her head tilting to the side as she regarded him. "Is everything all right? I couldn't help but overhear."

Marchand swept over to her, a slight furrow creasing his brow. "Ah, Lady Hawthorne. It appears the lady had simply misplaced her earrings." He paused, clasping his hands together in front of him with a measured shift of his weight. "You know, it is common for guests to be convinced that their valuable items have been stolen, only to realise when they return home that they had left them there all along."

Elizabeth's eyes narrowed as she studied Marchand's demeanour, her lips pursing in thoughtful. Though his smile remained, it lacked the easy confidence that typically characterised his interactions.

"It's easily done, I'm sure." Elizabeth's tone carried a note of cautious probing as she spoke. "I'm relieved to hear it was merely a misunderstanding." Her gaze remained trained on him, searching for any signs that might betray the true nature of the situation.

Something about Marchand's uncharacteristic tension made her unsure whether he was being entirely forthright.

Clearing his throat, Marchand's expression shifted to a more professional veneer. "Ah, yes, the telephone call you requested. I shall place that with the exchange at once and notify you as soon as it comes through."

He gave a slight incline of his head, the movement lacking its usual fluid grace. "If you'll excuse me, I'm afraid I must attend to a few other matters. Please, let me know if there's anything else I can do for you, Lady Elizabeth."

With that, Monsieur Marchand offered Elizabeth a thin, tight-lipped smile before turning and striding away, his steps carrying a subtle edge of haste.

Elizabeth's eyes narrowed slightly as she watched him go. Something about the interaction left her unsettled, but she pushed the concern aside. There were more pressing matters to attend to – clearing her cousin's name. Squaring her shoulders, she made her way to the lift. A plan already formulating in her mind.

Elizabeth opened the door to her suite. Aunt Beatrice sat rigid in her armchair, a newspaper crumpled in her lap. Her face, usually a mask of composure, had lost all colour.

"Elizabeth, is that you?" Aunt Beatrice called from her bedroom. "We've been frantic – I was just about to send Meli to search for you."

"Oh Aunt, I'm so sorry. I left a note about my walk, but in all the…" Her gaze fell to the newspaper, heart sinking as she spotted Alexander's photograph, accompanied by a scandalous French headline.

Elizabeth's heart sank.

Aunt Beatrice's grip tightened, knuckles paling as she threw the paper down onto the bed. "It's dreadful, Elizabeth."

She reached to give Aunt Beatrice's shoulder a gentle squeeze. "Perhaps we should call the doctor? You look quite unwell."

But Aunt Beatrice's dismissive wave cut her off. "Nonsense. I'm perfectly all right. It's Alexander we should be worrying about." Despite the firm words, Elizabeth couldn't help but notice the dark circles under her aunt's eyes, the way she kept twisting her lace handkerchief.

"You must do something, Elizabeth. Alexander's fate hangs by a thread. Once word reaches London, then we'll all be ruined." Her lips pursed, as if weighing her next words carefully. "I know I don't typically approve of your little adventures, but perhaps you could…"

"Of course, Aunt. I'll make some enquiries, see what I can find out."

She tried to make it sound as innocuous as possible. As if she were making enquiries about a new dress fabric or dish. There was no point worrying her aunt about the practicalities. The less she knew about the true nature of Elizabeth's adventures and what they entailed, the better.

Meli swept into the sitting room from the bedroom, her gaze landing on Elizabeth. "Elizabeth. There you are. You've been gone such a long time, we were worried about you." A flicker of relief passed across her features as her eyes searched Elizabeth's face. "Is everything all right?"

Elizabeth sank down beside her cousin, exhaling heavily. "I'm afraid not. Aunt Beatrice is quite distressed over this dreadful newspaper article." She paused, her expression turning serious. "Meli, there's something I didn't tell you yesterday, with all the upset over Alexander's arrest."

Meli swallowed hard. "Go on."

"Detective Lefèvre-"

Meli's brow knitted together, a shadow of indignation passing over her face. "Don't mention that wretched man's name! After the way he treated Alexander…" She trailed off, her jaw tightening visibly.

"Detective Lefèvre told me the chief inspector has been under pressure from the Mayor to make an arrest, and it seems Alexander is nothing more than a scapegoat."

Meli's eyes widened. "Surely he can't arrest someone without proper proof?"

"There's some very flimsy circumstantial evidence that he's using to buy time while he builds his case."

"That's outrageous." Meli's lips pressed into a thin line, anger burning in her eyes. "And I suppose Detective Lefèvre is party to this?"

"Hardly. He's been most helpful, all things considered. He told me if I want to clear Alexander's name, I need to find the evidence myself."

Meli huffed, a sceptical furrow creasing her brow. "Isn't that his job?"

"Usually yes, but with Chief Inspector Dubois convinced he has his man, he isn't looking for any other suspects." Elizabeth paused, then added with a sidelong glance at her cousin, "Detective Lefèvre asked after you."

Meli's lips pursed, though Elizabeth detected a flicker of interest in her cousin's eyes. "The nerve of him! As if I'd have anything to do with that horrid man after what he's done." But the petulant tone was undermined by the telltale twitch at the corner of her mouth.

Elizabeth gave Meli's arm a gentle squeeze. "I understand your feelings about Detective Lefèvre, but right now, we need to put them aside. Alexander's future is at stake, and we must focus on clearing his name, no matter the personal cost."

Meli let out an exaggerated sigh. "Oh, very well. I suppose I could try to be civil to him… but just for Alexander's sake."

Elizabeth turned to her cousin, her hand coming to rest on her arm. "Meli, I need you to do something for me."

"Of course, anything." Meli's face brightened, excitement dancing in her eyes.

"I need to search Princess Sofia's room again, but I'm concerned about Aunt Beatrice." Elizabeth glanced towards the bedroom. "Evelyn's with her, but you know how Aunt Beatrice can be when she's upset. Would you mind staying close?"

Meli's shoulders drooped, then squared. She met Elizabeth's gaze. "I'll stay with Aunt Beatrice." A pause. "And Elizabeth, if you need help with your investigation, I'm here. For more than just minding Aunt Beatrice, you know."

Elizabeth squeezed Meli's hand. "I know you're capable, Meli." She glanced towards the door, then back to her cousin. "But this situation… it's unpredictable. I'd feel better knowing you're safe here with Aunt Beatrice." Her lips curved into a small smile. "I won't be long."

Elizabeth retrieved her trusty lock picking kit from her bag and made her way towards the princess's suite. Pausing at the door, she cocked her head, watching and listening until she was certain the corridor lay empty. With a deft flick of her wrists, she coaxed the lock open and slipped inside, her senses instantly alert.

Silence filled the room, save for the faint creak of the floorboards beneath her feet. Elizabeth's gaze fell on the dark stain marring the lush carpet - a grim memento of the tragedy that had unfolded here. Steeling herself, she began her examination of the room.

Elizabeth's gloved fingers rested on the handles of the wardrobe doors as she pulled them open, her eyes widening at the lavish display within. An array of sumptuous evening gowns hung before her, but a single, dowdy day dress stood out amongst the sea of opulent fabrics. Curiously, not a hat or hat box was to be seen – an unusual oversight for a woman of the princess's standing.

Sifting through the hanging garments, Elizabeth paused as her fingertips brushed against the simple, utilitarian cut and coarse material of the day dress. What was this doing here, tucked away in the princess's wardrobe? Studying the other gowns more closely, she noted the stitching had a homemade quality, lacking the refined tailoring of true couture. These were clever imitations, expertly crafted to mimic the height of fashion, but the eagle-eyed fashionista could spot the subtle flaws.

Shifting her focus, Elizabeth crossed the room to the ornate chest of drawers. Grasping the handle of the top drawer, she pulled it open, revealing a sparse collection of silk stockings and delicate undergarments.

Turning her attention to the second drawer, Elizabeth tugged it open, only to find it empty. But as she tried to push it closed again, it stuck, refusing to close all the way. Frowning, she opened it and peered inside. Reaching in, Elizabeth's gloved fingers searched along the back, coming to rest on something soft. With a gentle tug, she pulled it free. Stifling a scream as a cascade of chestnut-coloured hair spilled across her palm.

Nothing was making sense, with each new find only compounding the perplexing questions swirling in Elizabeth's mind.

Brow furrowed, she ran her fingertips over the wig, marvelling at its fine, realistic texture. This was no mere costume piece – the quality of the hair was far too exceptional for that. But what was it doing stuffed in the back of the drawer?

As she contemplated the unsettling implications, a faint sound outside the door caught her attention. Elizabeth froze, pulse quickening as she strained to listen. Footsteps. Approaching the suite.

Elizabeth's heart hammered against her ribcage when the footsteps halted outside the door. Her eyes darted around the room, searching desperately for a hiding place.

Her breath hitched at the soft click of a key turning in the lock. Gripping the wig, she seized the brass handle of the French doors, rattling it in a frantic attempt to escape. With a gentle push, she slipped out onto the balcony just as the door swung open.

Peering through the glass, Elizabeth watched as a partially illuminated figure moved around the room, their identity obscured. The stranger's footsteps were hurried, frantic, as they began rummaging through the princess's belongings.

Straining to listen, she heard the intruder let out a frustrated huff, muttering curses in French as they moved from one place to another. Blood pounded in her ears, her thundering heart beats threatening to give her away at any moment.

Was this the princess's murderer, returning to the scene of the crime? The thought of a looming confrontation with a killer twisted her stomach in fear.

The shuffling footsteps neared the balcony, affording her a split-second glimpse of a pair of men's legs clad in the hotel's signature uniform trousers - black with a subtle maroon pinstripe running up the side seam. Elizabeth pressed herself against the wall, forcing herself to remain still and silent. Only two men wore that distinctive livery - the hotel manager, Monsieur Marchand, and his assistant.

Elizabeth's eyes widened as she recalled the guest's heated confrontation with the pair earlier that day. Had he been correct in his claim that one of the Majestique's staff was a jewellery thief?

She let out a shaky exhale as the retreating footsteps and the door closing signalled the intruder's departure. Turning to head back inside, her eyes honed in on the dark, rusty smear staining the railing. Heart pounding, she leaned closer, her fingers clutching the bougainvillea covered trellis for support.

The instant her weight settled, it gave a sudden lurch, the loose joints shifting beneath her.

But Elizabeth scarcely registered the precarious state of the trellis, her focus entirely consumed by the chilling implications of that bloodstain.

Had this been the site of the princess's brutal demise?

Chapter Eleven

ELIZABETH SWEPT INTO HER suite, her mind still reeling from the unsettling revelations she had uncovered in the princess's rooms. Meli looked up from her armchair, her brow creasing with curiosity.

"Elizabeth, whatever's the matter?" Meli rose, her movements hesitant.

Glancing towards Aunt Beatrice's closed door, Elizabeth lowered her voice. "Not here. I don't want Aunt Beatrice to hear."

Meli followed Elizabeth into their shared bedchamber, her footsteps quick and light. As she closed the door, she leaned against it, her eyes fixed on her cousin.

Elizabeth sank down onto the edge of her bed, her hands fidgeting in her lap as she recounted the unsettling discoveries she had made in the princess's rooms. The odd, incongruous assortment of garments. The mysterious intruder. And that smear of blood – all clues that hinted at something far bigger than she'd first thought.

Meli's jaw fell slack as Elizabeth finished speaking. She shook her head in disbelief. "I simply can't fathom it. Do you truly believe Monsieur Marchand or Monsieur Róbert might be involved somehow? Could they be working in tandem to conceal the truth?"

Elizabeth met Meli's gaze, her voice low. "I honestly don't know, Meli. But it's troubling. Guests complaining of missing jewellery, an intruder in the princess's room..." She paused. "And those trousers the intruder wore – they're the same as those worn by the hotel management."

Elizabeth looked towards the balcony. "There's something else, Meli. A smear of blood on the railings outside." She paused. "What if the princess wasn't murdered in her room? What if it happened on the balcony?"

Meli's eyes widened. "Do you think someone moved her body?" Meli asked, her eyes widening. But why on earth would they do that?"

Shaking her head slightly, Elizabeth considered the implications. "I'm not sure, but perhaps to hide the true location of the crime or in case someone spotted her out there."

"Goodness," Meli breathed, her expression growing more troubled. "The princess had some striking pieces. Do you think one or both of them murdered her for her jewellery? Perhaps she discovered them in the act, so they had to silence her?"

Elizabeth tilted her head slightly, considering Meli's words. "It's possible, I suppose, but if theft were the motive, why didn't they take the bracelet she was wearing or her earrings, not to mention the silver jewellery box?"

Meli's brow creased as she considered Elizabeth's words.

"But the princess's attire..." Elizabeth's voice drifted. "It almost felt as if..."

Meli leaned in, eyes alight with curiosity. "As if what, Elizabeth?"

Elizabeth's gaze searched Meli's face. "As if she wasn't really there. The lack of any personal belongings, her clothes. I know it's an odd thing to say, but it's almost as if that room was nothing more than … a dressing room…"

Meli leaned forward, her voice lowering. "Do you think the princess wasn't who she claimed to be?"

"It's possible," Elizabeth replied, her gaze drifting as her mind wandered back to her recent stay at Mayfield Manor and the Countess Von Habsfeld. "With all the upheaval in Europe after the Great War and Italy's complex history, the abundance of royal titles became ripe ground for potential impostors."

A sharp rap at the door pulled Elizabeth from her thoughts. Rising, she crossed the room and opened the door to find Evelyn standing there. "Has something happened to my aunt?" Elizabeth's voice was tight with worry.

Evelyn shook her head. "No, Lady Elizabeth. Your aunt is resting comfortably." She hesitated, then continued, "Forgive the interruption, but the concierge has just left word that your call to London is ready."

Elizabeth sighed in relief. "Thank you, Evelyn. Do you think we should summon the doctor, though? Just to be sure."

Evelyn's expression grew fond, yet tinged with a hint of exasperation. "I broached the subject, but you know how steadfastly stubborn Lady Beatrice can be. She won't entertain the idea."

Elizabeth smiled, painfully familiar with the challenge of persuading her indomitable aunt to do something she didn't agree with.

"I suggested a turn about the gardens," Evelyn continued. "You know how much enjoyment she finds in their beauty."

"Indeed she does." Elizabeth arched an enquiring brow. "Did she agree to it?"

Evelyn gave a regretful shake of her head. "I'm afraid not."

Elizabeth's tone softened with gentle pleading. "Please, Evelyn, keep me informed of any change. And thank you, as always, for taking such good care of my aunt."

Evelyn dipped into a slight curtsy, a faint blush warming her cheeks.

Elizabeth watched her leave, a familiar unease settling over her. Aunt Beatrice's self-imposed seclusion at Le Majestique was troubling enough, but the thought of her returning to the isolation of Hawthorne Hall after their holiday weighed heavily on Elizabeth's mind.

Their travels and visits to the family's Belgravia home typically brightened Aunt Beatrice's mood, the change of scenery and company offering a temporary respite. Yet despite repeated invitations from Elizabeth and her brother, Lord William Hawthorne, Aunt Beatrice remained steadfast in her refusal to extend her stays.

Elizabeth's thoughts turned to the family plot on the Hawthornshire estate. There, beneath the ancient oaks, lay Aunt Beatrice's husband and daughter. Perhaps, Elizabeth mused, the proximity to those quiet graves held Aunt Beatrice more firmly than any invitation ever could.

Meli looked up, curiosity sparking in her eyes. "Who was the call to?"

Glancing at the clock, Elizabeth replied, "A journalist friend of mine at *The Times* in London. I needed to find out if the British press has heard about Alexander's arrest." She stood, smoothing her skirt with deliberate motions. "I'd better speak to her."

Taking a deep breath, she stepped out of the suite and headed towards the lift. The hushed chatter and sidelong glances of other guests followed her across the foyer.

Approaching the reception desk, she met Monsieur Marchand's polished smile.

"Lady Elizabeth, your London call is ready in my office. You'll have complete privacy there."

Elizabeth nodded. "Thank you, Monsieur Marchand. That's most considerate."

Monsieur Marchand led Elizabeth to his office, away from the bustling reception. "I'll leave you to your call," he said, stepping out and closing the door.

Settling into the chair, Elizabeth lifted the receiver. "Cybil? It's Elizabeth Hawthorne. Thank you for returning my call."

As she discussed the matter of Alexander's arrest with Cybil, Elizabeth's attention drifted to the leather-bound guest register resting on Monsieur Marchand's desk. Casting a quick glance around to ensure the door was closed, she slid the book towards her, flipping the pages with a delicate touch.

A frown tugged at the corners of her mouth as she located the entry for Princess Sofia's suite – the room listed as unoccupied, with no guest name recorded. How very curious.

The sound of Monsieur Marchand's returning footsteps prompted Elizabeth to slide the register back into its original position.

With a short rap on the door, Monsieur Marchand re-entered. "I trust your business was concluded satisfactorily?" His gaze flicked towards the register before settling on her once more, his expression unreadable.

"Yes, thank you for the use of your office." Elizabeth inclined her head, trying to remain composed.

"Of course." Monsieur Marchand's lips curved in a polite smile. "Please, let me know if there's anything else I can do to make your stay more pleasant."

Elizabeth nodded. Had Monsieur Marchand noticed the register had been moved? Did he know she'd been perusing its contents?

Treading lightly would be paramount. The last thing Elizabeth wanted was to tip her hand and alert either man to her growing suspicions.

She breezed through the foyer, the whispered chatter of the other guests trailing in her wake. As she approached the lift, a familiar voice called out.

"Lady Elizabeth, a moment, if you please."

She turned to find Mr Gray striding towards her, a warm smile tugging at the corners of his mouth. His piercing blue gaze held a glimmer of concern as he drew near.

"Mr Gray." Elizabeth's brows arched slightly, a touch of surprise colouring her tone.

The lines around his eyes crinkled as his expression sobered. "I couldn't help but notice Lady Hawthorne's absence from our bridge game yesterday." His gaze searched her face, a furrow forming between his brows. "I must confess, I've been quite worried about her."

Elizabeth's features softened, a faint crease appearing between her own brows. "Ah, yes. I'm afraid my aunt has withdrawn to our suite since…" Her voice trailed off, the weight of the past day's events settling heavily on her shoulders.

Mr Gray fell silent for a moment, his fingers drumming against his trouser leg. Then, his eyes lit with a spark of inspiration. "Perhaps a friendly game of backgammon might lift her spirits? He angled in. "I'd be honoured to bring my set and pay her a visit, if you think she'd be amenable."

Elizabeth felt a surge of gratitude swell within her. "Why, Mr Gray, that's an exceptionally kind offer. My aunt adores a game of backgammon." She clasped her hands together, her fingers twining. "I'm certain a bit of friendly competition would do her the power of good."

Mr Gray's face brightened, the tension in his features easing. "Excellent. Then I shall make the necessary arrangements and call upon you all this afternoon." He dipped his head in a courteous nod.

Elizabeth inclined her head slightly. "We shall be most pleased to receive you, Mr Gray."

With a final warm smile, Mr Gray excused himself, his steps carrying him across the foyer and through the front doors.

Turning, Elizabeth made her way back to the suite. Perhaps this unexpected visit would be the pick-me-up Aunt Beatrice needed.

Elizabeth entered their suite, finding Aunt Beatrice gazing out the sitting-room window. The elder woman's usual equilibrium was somewhat off.

"Aunt Beatrice." Elizabeth approached the chair where her aunt sat. "How are you holding up?"

Aunt Beatrice's gaze remained fixed out the window, her lips pressed into a thin line. "As well as one can ... given the circumstances."

Settling into the chair opposite, Elizabeth studied her aunt. "I encountered Mr Gray downstairs. He expressed concern over your absence from the bridge game yesterday."

Aunt Beatrice's brow raised, a glimmer of curiosity igniting in her sapphire eyes.

"In fact, we've arranged for him to visit this afternoon for a game of backgammon." Elizabeth leaned forward, her voice lowering. "I thought a game might lift your spirits. Help take your mind off Alexander's situation."

Aunt Beatrice gave a dismissive flick of her hand. "I've no desire for company, least of all Mr Gray and his backgammon."

"I understand. I'll send word to cancel the arrangement." Elizabeth studied her aunt, noting the subtle shift in her demeanour.

Aunt Beatrice let out an exasperated huff, but the tightness in her expression eased. "Oh, very well. Since you've already made the arrangement, it would be discourteous to cancel at such short notice." Her piercing gaze flicked towards Elizabeth, the barest hint of amusement in her eyes. "But it was most presumptuous of you to make plans on my behalf, Elizabeth."

Aunt Beatrice rose from her chair, turning to her companion. "Come, Evelyn."

As they crossed the sitting room, a sharp, ear-splitting scream ripped through the air. Elizabeth's heart lurched, and she bolted from the room. "Meli!"

Chapter Twelve

ELIZABETH BURST INTO THE bedroom, the door slamming against the wall with a resounding crack. Meli pressed herself into the corner, her warm complexion drained to bone-white, toffee eyes stretched wide with terror. "Meli, whatever's the matter?" Elizabeth's gaze scanned the room, searching for any sign of immediate danger.

Meli's arm shot up, her trembling finger pointing to the floor. "A rat! There's a rat!" The words rushing out in a high-pitched shriek.

Elizabeth followed the line of Meli's gesture, her pulse quickening at the sight of the small, matted shape peeking out from beneath the bed. Meli's lips parted, a strangled cry tumbling out as she shrank further into the corner. "It moved, Elizabeth! I saw it move!"

"Girls, whatever's going on in there?" Aunt Beatrice's voice carried from the sitting room.

"There's a—" Meli's words wavered, high-pitched with alarm.

Elizabeth cut in. "It's nothing, Aunt. Just a ... spider, that's all."

With a flurry of dark curls, Meli dashed across the room, the ensuite door rattling shut behind her.

Elizabeth positioned herself between the en-suite and the mysterious object, her hazel gaze narrowing as she studied the matted fur. Something about the creature's stillness gave her pause. Glancing around, she spotted a poker resting in the hearth and wrapped her fingers around it, crouching down to investigate further.

Angling the metal rod, Elizabeth gave the suspicious shape a gentle prod. To her surprise, the *rat* refused to scurry away, remaining completely motionless. A faint chuckle passed her lips as she leaned in to inspect. "Why, this isn't a rat at all…" Her soothing tone beckoned to Meli. "Meli, you can come out now."

Slowly, the en-suite door cracked open, Meli's eyes darting between Elizabeth and the mysterious object. "Is it … dead?" A tremor ran through her words.

Elizabeth poked at the matted tangle of hair. "No, it's quite alive. Well, as alive as a wig can be, that is." She crossed the room in measured strides, coming to a halt before the ensuite.

Meli emerged, sweeping an apprehensive glance towards Elizabeth's outstretched hand. "A wig? Whatever's it doing here?"

Elizabeth canted her head, presenting the wig for closer inspection. She turned it over in her hands, her gaze narrowing as she recalled the events in the suite. "I discovered it jammed in the back of a drawer in the princess's suite." She glanced at Meli, then back at the wig. "I must have tucked it into my pocket when I fled the intruder, and it seems to have slipped out without my notice."

Meli's brow furrowed as she leaned in, eyes gleaming with curiosity. "Do you think it belonged to the princess?"

"I can only assume so." Elizabeth's lips pursed, a thoughtful crease appearing between her brows. "Unless it was overlooked by housekeeping and belonged to a previous guest, but I highly doubt that to be the case at Le Majestique."

Meli's fingers traced the delicate strands, her brow furrowing in thought. Suddenly, her eyes lit up with realisation. "Elizabeth, don't you remember what you said earlier? About the princess's suite feeling almost like a dressing room?"

Elizabeth's gaze sharpened, her head inclining in a slow, deliberate nod. "Yes, you're right. That might explain the discordant day-dress hanging in the wardrobe, completely out of place alongside the evening gowns." She paused, holding the wig up to the light. "Do you think the princess was putting on some sort of show? That she wasn't really who she claimed to be?"

"It's certainly beginning to look that way." Meli's gaze lingered on the wig.

Elizabeth examined it more closely, noting the fine workmanship. "The hair quality is quite exceptional."

Meli leaned in. "And the styling – the waves and curls seem very natural." She studied the soft strands, a thoughtful expression on her face.

Parting the wig, Elizabeth spotted an embroidered label. "*Madame Delphine - Cannes*," she read aloud.

Meli tapped her chin thoughtfully. "I think we should speak to this Madame Delphine. If the princess bought the wig from her, she may know something useful."

Elizabeth nodded. "Yes, I agree. This wig could provide a clue about the princess and whether she was who she claimed to be." She met Meli's eyes. "Let's find Madame Delphine and see what she can tell us."

Elizabeth's gaze met Meli's. "I believe we should start by speaking with the concierge. He may be able to provide us with the address for Madame Delphine's shop."

Meli's head dipped in a measured nod. "Yes, good idea."

Elizabeth eased the wig into a paper bag, tucking it into her clutch. She and Meli made their way to the sitting room, side by side. As they entered, Mr Gray rose from his seat.

"Lady Elizabeth, Mademoiselle Diomaros," he greeted them with a smile. "Won't you be joining us this afternoon?"

Elizabeth responded with an apologetic smile. "Unfortunately, Meli and I have some pressing matters to attend to. Another time, perhaps."

Mr Gray's eyebrow raised. "Ah, I understand. If you need any assistance, please don't hesitate to ask."

Aunt Beatrice's voice rang out. "Elizabeth, are you looking into Alexander's situation? My niece is quite the detective, you know, Mr Gray. I have the utmost faith she'll soon uncover the evidence to exonerate him.""

"Is that so? Mr Gray's interest visibly piqued.

Elizabeth's lips curved in a faint, self-deprecating smile. "My aunt is grossly exaggerating my talents."

"Nonsense, child!" Aunt Beatrice flicked a dismissive hand. "Who was it solved that ghastly murder on your return voyage from Athens? Not to mention that dreadful business with the Mayfields."

Elizabeth cast a pointed look at her aunt, willing her to silence. "We really must be going, Aunt Beatrice. Come, Meli."

Once they were in the corridor, Meli turned to Elizabeth. "I thought Aunt Beatrice didn't approve of your *adventures*, as she calls them."

"Typically, she doesn't." Elizabeth exchanged a puzzled glance with Meli. Aunt Beatrice's enthusiastic description of her detective work, especially in front of acquaintances, was entirely out of character.

They descended to the foyer in the lift. As they stepped out, Elizabeth guided her cousin towards the concierge's desk.

Elizabeth approached the concierge with a polite smile. "Pardon me, Monsieur. My cousin and I were hoping you might assist us. Do you happen to know the location of Madame Delphine's shop?"

Recognition flickered in the concierge's eyes, his moustache twitching as he offered a discreet smile. "*Me oui*, I believe I know the establishment you're referring to." He leaned in slightly. "Madame Delphine caters to some of our most distinguished guests."

Meli stepped forward. "We would be most grateful if you could provide the address."

"But of course." The concierge jotted down the details, presenting the card to Elizabeth.

She accepted it with a gracious nod. "Thank you. You've been most helpful." With a smile, Elizabeth discreetly pressed a gratuity into his palm.

The concierge's expression brightened, but his smile quickly faded as Monsieur Marchand appeared beside them, his keen eyes taking in the scene.

"Lady Elizabeth, Mademoiselle Diomaros. I trust my staff have been attending to your needs?"

Elizabeth met his gaze, her fingers curling around her clutch. "Indeed, Monsieur Marchand. Your concierge has been most helpful."

Marchand's brow arched, a hint of suspicion colouring his tone. "May I inquire about your plans for the afternoon? Perhaps I can be of assistance."

"Just a few personal matters to attend to, thank you. We'll manage." She met his gaze evenly, unwilling to reveal more.

With a polite nod, Elizabeth turned and she and Meli made their way towards the front door.

Elizabeth and Meli made their way along the Boulevard de la Croisette, weaving through the mid-morning crowd of tourists and locals. As they walked, Elizabeth's gaze flicked between passing faces and shop fronts, her mind clearly at work.

"We'll pose as friends of the princess," Elizabeth murmured, her eyes meeting Meli's. "Referring to her only as our dear friend. That should avoid raising suspicion if Madame Delphine knows her by another name."

Meli's lips curved into a conspiratorial smile. "And we'll express our admiration for the wig's quality, claiming we'd like one just like it. That should let us gather information without drawing unwanted attention."

As they approached *Rue d'Antibes*, the elegant façade of Madame Delphine's shop came into view. Elizabeth's eyes scanned the tasteful window displays, hinting at the craftsmanship within. The chime of the brass bell announced their arrival, and a woman of sophistication and poise greeted them.

Madame Delphine's piercing blue-grey eyes swept over them, her perfectly arched brows lifting. "Welcome to my shop, *mesdames*. I am Madame Delphine." Her cultured voice carried a hint of a Parisian accent. "How can I assist you today?"

Elizabeth offered a warm smile. "*Bonjour*, Madame Delphine. I'm Elizabeth, and this is my cousin, Meli." She gestured to Meli, who dipped her head in a polite greeting. Elizabeth extracted the wig from her clutch, placing it on the counter. "I was speaking to a dear friend about needing a ... change, and she suggested you might be able to help."

Elizabeth chose not to use her title, knowing it often made people uneasy. She wanted to keep things informal, hoping Madame Delphine would feel comfortable enough to share more freely.

Madame Delphine's narrowed gaze settled on Elizabeth, then shifted to the wig. Delicate fingers caressed the soft chestnut strands. "This is one of my creations. I remember it well." She paused, her nose twitching. "What are you doing with it?"

Elizabeth's mind raced to find the right words. "I admired it so much that my friend allowed me to borrow it. I was hoping you could create something similar for me."

Madame Delphine's brow pinched as she tossed the wig back down onto the counter, Elizabeth's heart sinking. "Non, I am an artist. Every one of my pieces is unique, an original." Her chin lifted with a flicker of pride.

Elizabeth infused her tone with admiration, hoping to persuade. "The craftsmanship is truly exceptional. That's exactly why I sought you out. My friend said your work is the finest in all of France."

A faint smile tugged at the corner of Madame Delphine's mouth. "Perhaps I can accommodate your request." She paused, appraising Elizabeth. "What did you have in mind, mademoiselle?"

Thinking on her feet, Elizabeth chose a colour far from her natural shade. "How about blonde? Something completely different."

Madame Delphine's keen gaze studied Elizabeth, a thoughtful hum escaping her. "Yes, I believe a lovely golden blonde would suit you perfectly." She retrieved a small swatch of hair, holding it up to Elizabeth's face. "This shade, perhaps? Though I must warn you, the finished creation may not be an exact match – each of my pieces is a unique, one-of-a-kind work."

As the shopkeeper made her assessment, Elizabeth seized the opportunity. "I'm sure your services must be in high demand, Madame."

"Oh, but of course." Madame Delphine's nimble fingers began measuring Elizabeth's head. "Actresses are some of my most frequent patrons. But I also cater to the more fashionable ladies of Cannes who desire a certain *je ne sais quoi*."

Meli's casual tone drew the shopkeeper's focus. "And do these ladies often visit you in person to be fitted?"

"*Mais oui*." Madame Delphine nodded, her gaze never leaving her work. "I find it essential to meet with each client, to ensure the perfect fit and styling." She paused, glancing up at Meli. "Though I must say, some of my more ... private clients prefer discreet fittings at their residences."

Elizabeth and Meli exchanged a subtle glance. "And what about my friend? Did she visit you here?"

"Yes, I remember her well." The shopkeeper's lips pursed thoughtfully. "An American, exquisitely dressed in the latest fashion and dripping in fine jewellery. I must say, it surprised me when she requested the wig to be delivered to a caisse postale rather than her home address.

Elizabeth's eyes widened. "A *caisse postale*?"

Madame Delphine nodded, her fingers continuing their work. "*Oui*, she claimed her home was undergoing renovations, and she was renting a *caisse postale* while travelling." The shopkeeper's brow arched.

Meli's lips curved into a faint smile as Elizabeth replied, "Of course, it must have been when she was visiting her sister." The lie fell from Elizabeth's lips. "Madame, I don't suppose you remember the location of the post office, do you? I've been looking for a discreet way to have some private documents delivered, things I'd prefer my husband not know about."

Madame Delphine's expression softened with understanding. "But of course. Let me consult my records." She turned to her order book, quickly locating the relevant information. "The *caisse postale* is on the *Rue de Rivoli*, just a short distance from here."

As she relayed the details to Elizabeth, Meli scanned the columns where Madame Delphine's finger paused, committing the caisse postale number to memory without drawing attention.

Madame Delphine completed her measurements with a flourish, setting her tools aside. "Very well, madame. I believe I have everything I need to create something exquisite for you."

Elizabeth nodded. "How long will it take to complete? I can hardly wait."

Madame Delphine tapped her chin as she pondered, her eyes scanning Elizabeth's features. "Given my current schedule, it should take no more than two weeks. I pride myself on meticulous craftsmanship, so I assure you, it will be worth the wait."

"Thank you, madame. That sounds perfect."

"Would you like me to arrange for it to be delivered?"

"No, I will collect it myself." Elizabeth kept her tone light, mindful of her earlier comments about needing a local *caisse postale*. It wouldn't do to admit she was staying at Le Majestique.

"*Très bien*," Madame Delphine replied, satisfaction clear in her nod. She took a piece of headed paper and scribbled some figures on it before folding it and sliding it across the desk to Elizabeth.

Elizabeth read the numbers, then reached into her purse, producing the full payment and placing it on the counter. "Thank you very much, Madame Delphine."

Madame Delphine accepted the payment with a slight, almost imperceptible nod. "*Merci beaucoup*, madame. It's been a pleasure doing business with you."

Elizabeth and Meli murmured their thanks, then stepped out onto the bustling *Rue d'Antibes*. Elizabeth's gaze flicked to her wristwatch, a frustrated sigh escaping her. "It's too late to visit the post office now. We'll have to go first thing tomorrow."

The two women fell into step, making their way back towards Le Majestique. As they walked, Meli's brow furrowed as she scrutinised Elizabeth's expression. "So, the princess was American, not Italian, as she claimed. Why would she go to such lengths to conceal her true identity? And the *caisse postale* – it doesn't add up. If she'd been staying at Le Majestique, why didn't she have her purchases delivered there?" Meli's gaze drifted to the sparkling sea, a frown tugging at her lips.

Elizabeth's bewilderment mirrored Meli's. "In my experience, Meli, those who disguise their identity usually have something to hide. But this whole affair… " She shook her head, frustration tightening her features. "It's as if the more we uncover, the less it makes sense. The fake identity, the dichotomy of handmade clothes and fabulous gems…"

Meli's shoulders slumped, a weary sigh escaping her. "It's maddening. We thought

Madame Delphine would provide answers, but all she's done is open up a Pandora's box."

Dread coiled in Elizabeth's chest as her eyes narrowed. Chief Inspector Dubois had made it clear he was in no doubt of Alexander's guilt, more concerned with preserving Cannes' pristine façade than pursuing the truth. If Elizabeth didn't uncover the evidence to exonerate Alexander, his liberty – and their family's hard-earned reputation – would be utterly ruined.

Yet the prospect of continuing this treacherous investigation filled her with trepidation. The princess's web of deception had already cost one life – what other dangers might they be courting by delving deeper?

But she owed it to Alexander, to their family, to see this through. If the authorities wouldn't act, then she and Meli had no choice but to continue their search, to unravel the mystery of the princess's true identity, no matter the personal risk.

Peril or not, she couldn't turn away – not when so much was at stake.

Chapter Thirteen

OUTSIDE THE POST OFFICE on *Rue de Rivoli*, Meli watched in astonishment as Elizabeth retrieved a slim, gilded tube from her purse. With precise, practiced motions, she applied a slick of bold crimson lipstick, studying her reflection with a critical eye. Giving her lashes a delicate flutter, she let out a girlish giggle before pushing through the front doors.

Approaching the counter, Elizabeth offered the clerk a bright, effortless smile. "Pardon me, monsieur." She heaved out an exaggerated sigh, her brow creasing with feigned distress. "I'm afraid I'm a little lost. I've just arrived from Paris to stay with my cousin, but I must have taken a wrong turn somewhere." Leaning in slightly, Elizabeth gave the clerk an apologetic look. "Would you be an absolute gem and give me some directions to her apartment? I have the address right here in my purse."

Without warning, Elizabeth's purse spilled open, the contents scattering across the floor. "Oh no, I'm so clumsy." Her eyes went wide. "Everything's going wrong today. The clasp on my purse broke, then I lost my ticket…" Dropping to her knees, she began scooping up the scattered items, shooting the flustered clerk an apologetic glance. "And now I've lost the piece of paper with her address." Her eyes filled with tears.

The clerk hurried around the counter to assist her. Elizabeth rewarded him with a flutter of her lashes. "You're so kind, thank you," she breathed, her voice softening.

Once the last stray item had been retrieved, Elizabeth got to her feet, the clerk gripping her elbow and helping her towards a chair with a delicate touch. "I've come all this way from Paris, and now I've lost her address. What am I going to do? Where will I stay?" Her brow creased with exaggerated concern.

"Do you remember the name of the street?" The clerk tugged at his shirt collar.

"No," Elizabeth shuddered. "But I know she has a caisse postale at this post office, because I've sent her letters here."

"The caisse postale number, Mademoiselle?" the clerk inquired.

Elizabeth recited it promptly, her eyes following the clerk as he disappeared among the shelves of records.

When he returned with the address, Elizabeth sprang to her feet, a dazzling smile blossoming on her lips. "Oh, you're an absolute angel!" Her eyes sparkled with delight. "I don't know what I would have done without you. Thank you, truly."

With a final grateful smile, Elizabeth hurried out to rejoin Meli, who greeted her with an amused chuckle. "Encore," Meli teased. "That was quite the performance."

The narrow, winding streets felt claustrophobic as Elizabeth and Meli hurried along, the address scribbled on a slip of paper clutched in Elizabeth's hand. This was a far cry from the grand boulevards and glamorous shops frequented by the elite.

Meli's eyes darted from one weather-worn apartment building to the next. "Elizabeth, are you absolutely certain this is the right place? Surely someone of the princess's claimed rank could never live in an area like this."

Elizabeth's pace quickened. "I believe we've already established the princess was not who she purported to be." Rounding a sharp corner, she paused, her gaze landing on a modest apartment building, squeezed between a bustling bakery and a small tobacco shop. "There, that must be it."

Meli hesitated, her teeth worrying at her lower lip. "Elizabeth, I'm not sure about this." She laid a gentle hand on her cousin's arm, her touch beseeching.

"You can wait here if you like, but I'm going to take a look." Elizabeth offered a reassuring smile. "We've come this far. We can't turn back now."

"I'm not letting you go in alone. What if the princess – or whoever she was – didn't live here alone?"

"Then I'll have to keep my wits about me." Straightening her shoulders, Elizabeth led the way into the building, Meli close behind. The poorly lit stairwell curved upwards, the stale, tobacco-tinged air giving the cramped space an ominous, oppressive feeling as muffled sounds of everyday life filtered through the walls. Climbing the stairs, their eyes flicked left and right at every creak and groan.

Elizabeth glanced at the apartment number scrawled on the slip of paper, then up at the row of doors. Her gaze paused on the princess's door. It stood ajar, a thin sliver of light visible in the gap.

Exchanging a wary glance, the cousins eased the door open and stepped inside, the sparse furnishings and humble decor a stark contrast to the opulence of Le Majestique. Meli's eyes widened as she took in the surroundings.

A sudden movement from the corner startled them, and they turned to see a shadowy figure rifling through the princess's belongings. Meli's sharp gasp cut through the silence, sending the intruder into a blind panic. Racing towards the open window, he sprang up onto the ledge.

He balanced precariously as if weighing his options, one hand grasping the wooden frame as the morning light glinted off the distinctive gold and onyx signet ring on his pinky finger.

Without warning, he pushed off the ledge, disappearing from sight.

They rushed to the window, watching as he made his escape over the tiled rooves below.

Meli's fingers tightened around the windowsill, her knuckles paling. "Who do you think that was?"

Elizabeth surveyed the room, eyes landing on the untouched jewellery. "I've no idea."

"Do you think he was a burglar?" Meli's voice wavered.

Elizabeth shook her head. "No, he was searching for something specific."

Meli's head tilted, puzzled. "Why do you say that?"

Elizabeth nodded towards the valuables, her eyes narrowing. "A burglar wouldn't ignore these."

Meli's eyes widened, her lips parting in a silent gasp. "Do you think they are real?"

Elizabeth held the diamond necklace to the light, tracing its facets. "There's one way to find out. She drew the stone across the rim of a brandy glass. It sliced through without resistance, leaving a faint, silvery line on the crystal. "Yes, it's most definitely real."

Meli leaned in, studying the necklace with a mix of awe and disbelief. "But ... who would leave something so valuable just lying around? And how can someone living here afford genuine diamonds?"

Elizabeth took a deep breath, her gaze sweeping the room. "This proves one thing."

"What?" Meli pressed, leaning forward.

Elizabeth replaced the necklace, her brow furrowed in concentration. "Whoever the intruder was, he was looking for something else." She straightened, pointing to the scattered jewellery. "Who leaves behind something like this if it's a simple theft?"

Meli nodded slowly, her fingers drumming against her thigh. "What do you think they were looking for?"

Elizabeth took a deep breath and met Meli's gaze. "I'm not sure what he was after, but he fled when we interrupted him. Let's split up and search the other rooms. Whatever he wanted might still be here."

Elizabeth navigated the cramped, cluttered apartment, noting the sink overflowing with dishes and the stale scent of old coffee in the air. As she rifled through a drawer, her hand stilled upon finding several identity documents, each bearing a different name and nationality. Her pulse quickened.

"Meli, look at these," she said, handing the documents to her cousin.

Meli's eyes widened, her face pale. "She had multiple identities. Who was she really?"

Elizabeth's fingers traced the edges of the forged papers. "This proves the princess was hiding more than we thought. She was living a web of lies." Realising the potential danger and importance of these documents, Elizabeth tucked them into her bag. "These could be crucial in uncovering the truth and clearing Alexander's name."

The weight of the discovery lingered in the air as Elizabeth moved into the living area, which doubled as a bedroom.

In one corner, an unmade put-me-up bed lay with tangled sheets and askew pillows. Her gaze landed on a stray earring glinting by the wardrobe. She picked it up, holding it to the light and turning it slowly. It was a very convincing fake. She pocketed the earring and moved to the wardrobe, where day dresses hung neatly, though some had slipped and bunched on the floor.

A mannequin head with an auburn wig of inferior quality to Madame Delphine's creation caught her eye.

A faint, sharp chemical smell lingered in the air.

"Elizabeth." Meli's urgent voice echoed from the bedroom. "I think you need to see this."

Elizabeth hurried across the hallway and stopped at the doorway. Instead of a bedroom, she found a cluttered workshop. A sturdy workbench dominated one corner, flanked by storage cabinets brimming with tools and materials. Meli's gaze swept over the array of pliers, files, and hammers neatly arranged. A small, portable electroplating kit sat in another corner, wires and electrodes poised for use. Nearby, a compact polishing wheel sat, ready to bring a shine to the finished pieces.

Meli turned to Elizabeth, eyes wide. "What is all this?"

Elizabeth lifted a worn magnifying glass from the workbench, its handle smooth from frequent use. She swept her gaze over the meticulously arranged tools and materials, then bent to examine a half-finished piece.

"It looks like the princess was involved in a counterfeit jewellery operation." Elizabeth's brow furrowed as she turned the piece over in her hand. "She's been creating these replicas, likely to replace genuine articles she no doubt acquired through her criminal contacts."

Meli's expression shifted from curiosity to alarm. "Good heavens, do you think the princess was involved in the jewellery thefts at Le Majestique?"

Elizabeth scanned the room, taking in the various tools and partially completed jewellery pieces. "It seems likely. My guess is she's working with someone at the hotel. When guests place valuables in the safe, the accomplice steals the jewellery and passes it to the princess, who makes copies to replace the originals."

Meli's brow furrowed. "Do you think her accomplice is Monsieur Marchand or Monsieur Róbert? That would explain their appearance in the princess's room."

"Remember the guest who complained about his wife's stolen jewellery?" Elizabeth asked. Meli nodded. "Maybe Monsieur Marchand and Monsieur Róbert were searching the princess's room for those missing pieces."

"It seems the princess has been leading a double life," Meli mused. "Should we inform the police?"

Elizabeth shook her head. "No ... not yet. Not until we've secured the evidence to clear Alexander."

The workshop felt cramped, tools and materials strewn about. Meli squeezed past a standing lamp perched precariously atop a set of drawers. As she brushed against it, the lamp wobbled.

"Careful, Meli!" Elizabeth warned.

Too late. The lamp toppled, crashing to the floor with a loud clatter. The shade dislodged, and a rolled-up piece of canvas tumbled out.

"Elizabeth, look at this!" Meli exclaimed, picking it up.

Elizabeth stepped closer, eyes widening. "This looks very much like a John Singer Sargent," she murmured, recognising the style from Aunt Beatrice's collection at Hawthorne Hall.

Meli's eyes widened. "Why would something like this be hidden in a lamp in the princess's apartment? Do you think this is what the intruder was after?"

Elizabeth inspected the painting, her mind racing. "If it's an original, it would be quite valuable," she said thoughtfully. "But I know someone who might be able to tell us more." Her expression brightened. "Monsieur Felix Bouchér."

Elizabeth's mind spun with everything they'd discovered about the princess. A web of lies, counterfeit jewellery, a hidden painting – how deep did the deception run? The princess wasn't just living a double life; she was orchestrating a grand scheme. And who was involved? Monsieur Marchand? Monsieur Róbert ?

A police siren wailed in the distance, jolting Elizabeth from her thoughts. The reality of their situation struck her hard – they had broken into a dead woman's apartment.

Meli's hand shot out, gripping Elizabeth's wrist. "Elizabeth," she whispered, "we need to leave."

Elizabeth nodded, a knot tightening in her stomach. They had to get out before anyone discovered them. As they slipped out the door, Elizabeth's mind raced with questions and an unwavering determination to uncover the truth.

Chapter Fourteen

THE JOURNEY FROM THE princess's apartment to Boulevard de la Croisette felt like a gauntlet. Every snap and shuffle set their hearts racing, certain they were being followed.

Elizabeth gripped Meli's arm, urging her to quicken their pace down the winding streets. Had the mysterious intruder given chase? Were there accomplices waiting in the shadows to silence them? Elizabeth's mind flew through the scenarios, her pulse thundering in her ears.

Rounding a corner, Elizabeth subtly adjusted the painting tucked securely inside her coat, its presence a constant reminder of the perilous situation they found themselves in. The sound of hurried footsteps approached from behind, and Meli shot Elizabeth a panicked look, neither daring to turn or slow their pace.

The footsteps grew louder, closer. Now he was beside them, and Elizabeth braced herself, prepared to fight if need be. She drew in a sharp breath, the aroma of freshly baked bread filling her nostrils.

"Bonjour, mesdames," the young man dressed in a baker's apron greeted as he passed, balancing a teetering stack of wicker baskets destined for the cafés and restaurants along the way.

Meli let out a shaky laugh, the tension easing a little in her shoulders. "Every little sound is making me jump," she admitted, casting an anxious glance over her shoulder. "I don't know about you, but I'll feel a lot safer when we're back at Le Majestique."

Elizabeth nodded, her own nerves still raw. "I agree, but even then, we mustn't let our guard down, Meli. After everything we've learned about the princess and the things she was involved in, we can't afford to trust anyone."

The oppressive atmosphere of the backstreets melted away as they stepped into Le

Majestique's grand foyer. The familiar bustle of well-heeled guests and attentive staff enveloped them.

Monsieur Marchand strode towards them, shoulders squared and chin lifted. "Lady Elizabeth, Mademoiselle Diomaros." He inclined his head. "I trust your morning's excursion was pleasant?"

Elizabeth smoothed a fold in her skirt. "Indeed, Monsieur Marchand. I couldn't help but notice earlier – has the matter with the gentleman's wife's jewellery been resolved satisfactorily?"

A flicker of something—perhaps surprise?—passed across Marchand's face before his professional mask slipped back into place. "Ah, yes. A regrettable misunderstanding, I'm pleased to say. The lady, it transpires, had not brought the piece in question on her travels. A telephone call to her household confirmed as much."

Elizabeth studied him, noting the slight tension in his shoulders, the way his fingers twitched almost imperceptibly. "How fortunate," she murmured, her gaze holding an unmistakable edge despite the genuine sympathy in her voice. "The anguish of losing a cherished memento must be quite unbearable."

Monsieur Marchand shifted uncomfortably, tugging at his collar.

Her smile was saccharine. "Now, if you'll excuse us, Monsieur, my aunt is expecting us for lunch."

He inclined his head, the tension in his shoulders betraying his unease. "Of course, bon appétit."

As they swept past him, Elizabeth felt Meli's questioning gaze, but she kept her focus trained ahead. Every interaction with Monsieur Marchand was a delicate dance, each word and gesture a potential clue in unravelling the mystery. She couldn't afford to let her guard down, not when so much was at stake.

The moment they entered the suite, Aunt Beatrice's voice cut through the air. "Elizabeth, is that you?"

Elizabeth inhaled sharply, gripping the rolled canvas beneath her coat. "Yes, Aunt." Aunt Beatrice rose from her chair, her movements sharp and agitated.

"Where have you two been?" Beatrice's brow pinched as her steely gaze flicked between the cousins. "I was starting to worry."

Elizabeth's expression tensed, the furrow of her brow and the downward pull of her lips betraying the weight of their discoveries. "Aunt, we need to talk. We've uncovered something quite troubling, and I think you should sit down."

Aunt Beatrice's lips pressed into a thin line, her fingers clenching the lace handkerchief in her lap. "Troubling? In what way?" Unease flickered in her eyes.

Meli glanced sidelong at Elizabeth, her toffee-coloured gaze brimming with unspoken concern. "It's about the princess, Aunt. She wasn't who she claimed to be."

Aunt Beatrice's chin lifted, a flicker of denial tightening her expression. "Nonsense, the princess was—"

"An imposter, Aunt." Elizabeth's words cut through Aunt Beatrice's protest, sharp and unyielding. "Everything about her identity was a lie."

Aunt Beatrice sank back into the chair, her eyes widening as the revelation sank in. "An imposter?" Her voice wavered.

Elizabeth moved to her aunt's side. "Are you all right?" She cast a worried glance at Evelyn. "Could you fetch some water?"

Aunt Beatrice waved a dismissive hand. "I'm fine, don't fuss." Her piercing gaze locked onto Elizabeth. "Well, if she wasn't a princess, then who was she?"

Elizabeth and Meli exchanged a heavy look, the tension palpable. "That's just it, Aunt. We don't know."

Aunt Beatrice's brow furrowed, confusion etching over her features. "Then how can you be sure she was an imposter?"

Handing her coat to Meli, Elizabeth settled into the chair across from Beatrice. She laid out the identity documents on the table. "We found these at the princess's apartment."

Aunt Beatrice picked up one of the papers, tutting as she scrutinised the information. With a shake of her head, she tossed it back down. "And how did you come by this?" She held up a halting hand. "No, perhaps it's better I don't know."

"That's not the worst of it," Elizabeth murmured, her teeth worrying her lower lip.

Aunt Beatrice's eyes narrowed. "You mean there's more?"

Elizabeth's solemn nod confirmed it. "We believe the princess was part of an elaborate jewellery counterfeiting scheme."

Colour drained from Aunt Beatrice's face, her knuckles paling as she clutched the handkerchief. "Good heavens, this is … dreadful." Her gaze darted between the cousins, a thread of panic lacing her words. "Poor Alexander. Thank goodness we learned the truth before he married her." Pleading eyes found Elizabeth's. "You must inform the police at once, clear his name before his reputation is ruined!"

Elizabeth released a weary sigh. "As incriminating as this is, Aunt, it doesn't prove Alexander's innocence."

Aunt Beatrice's shoulders sagged, the lines around her eyes deepening with worry. "But surely … this woman was a criminal."

"I'm afraid Chief Inspector Dubois will need something more definitive - an alibi or evidence pointing to another suspect."

Elizabeth reached out, giving her aunt's trembling hand a reassuring squeeze. "Meli and I will find a way to clear Alexander's name, Aunt. I promise."

The air around the luncheon table had been heavy, the revelations about the false princess leaving them all with little appetite. Elizabeth had barely touched her sandwich, her mind consumed by the need to uncover the truth.

As they prepared to leave, Elizabeth turned to Meli. "The painting—it's safely hidden? I'd rather not give Aunt Beatrice another worry before we speak to Monsieur Bouchér."

Meli nodded, a faint smile crossing her face. "Yes, it's hidden where she won't find it." Her expression grew more serious. "I do hope Clara doesn't miss our tennis lesson today. Mrs Hicks mentioned she was feeling unwell last night."

Elizabeth squeezed Meli's arm reassuringly. "I'm sure Clara will be feeling better by this afternoon." She glanced at the clock on the mantel, a hint of urgency creeping into her movements. "As for me, I'd better hurry if I want to get to the police station."

Meli leaned in, her voice low. "Do you think he's really forgotten where he was when the princess was murdered, or is he protecting someone?"

Elizabeth's gaze sharpened. "The latter, I suspect. If only he'd confide in me."

Stepping into the sitting room, they found Mr Gray and Aunt Beatrice absorbed in a game of backgammon. Gray glanced up, his eyes crinkling at the corners. "Lady Elizabeth, Miss Diomaros, I was hoping you would join us this afternoon, but I see Miss Diomaros is destined for the tennis courts. His gaze lingered on Elizabeth, a hint of curiosity in his eyes. "And you, Lady Elizabeth? Will you be joining her?"

Elizabeth offered him a polite smile. "Unfortunately, not today. I have a pressing matter to attend to."

Mr Gray arched a brow as if he sensed there was more to her excursion than she was letting on. "Is there anything I can do to help?" He inclined his head, his tone light.

"Thank you, no, Mr Gray, it's a rather personal matter."

"Well, then, I shan't keep you."

With a last exchange of farewells, Elizabeth and Meli departed the sitting room, travelling down together in the lift.

They parted ways in the foyer, each focused on their respective tasks – Meli heading out to the tennis courts, and Elizabeth steeling herself for her visit to the police station.

The journey to the station passed in a blur. Before Elizabeth knew it, she was stepping out of the taxi, her gaze immediately drawn to Chief Inspector Dubois exiting the police station wearing his customary scowl. She paused, ducking her head slightly to avoid his attention. Overhead, the once-bright sky had become hazy. The sunlight filtered through a veil of growing cloud cover.

As soon as he disappeared from view, Elizabeth made her way inside, slipping past the distracted desk sergeant.

The air within felt stifling, the scents of cigarette smoke and stale coffee mingling unpleasantly. Elizabeth fought the urge to wrinkle her nose as she made her way through the bustling office, her temples beginning to throb with the oppressive heat.

Detective Lefèvre's brow furrowed when he saw her. Excusing himself from the officer he'd been speaking with, he approached her.

"Lady Elizabeth," he greeted, keeping his voice low.

Elizabeth's gaze flicked across the crowded room, feeling the stifling air weigh on her.

Detective Lefèvre's eyes narrowed as he studied her. "I see." He gestured towards the exit. "Perhaps we should continue this conversation outside."

Outside, the air was only marginally cooler, but the humidity still clung to her skin. Detective Lefèvre's expression darkened as he turned to face her. "I take it you're here to inquire about any developments in Lord Cavendish's case?"

Elizabeth nodded. "Are you any closer to finding the actual murderer?"

A low rumble of thunder sounded in the distance as Detective Lefèvre spoke. "I'm afraid Chief Inspector Dubois remains convinced that Lord Cavendish is the actual murderer." A flicker of sympathy crossed his features as he paused. "Dubois's been looking into Lord Cavendish's finances and has found some ... information that only furthers his convictions."

Elizabeth's pulse quickened. "What sort of information?"

Reluctance flickered in Detective Lefèvre's gaze as he averted his eyes. "It seems Lord Cavendish has been selling off family assets – paintings, jewellery – to pay off his debts in England." He paused, choosing his words carefully. "Dubois believes Lord Cavendish attached himself to the princess, seeing her as a way to settle his financial troubles."

Elizabeth's composure fractured, her heart sinking. "But that's absurd!" The words tumbled out, tinged with disbelief. "If Alexander needed the princess's money, why would he kill her?"

Detective Lefèvre's expression grew sombre. "Dubois thinks there may have been a confrontation, a drunken argument that spiralled out of control – perhaps Lord Cavendish lashed out."

"That's ridiculous," Elizabeth protested, her brow furrowed in disbelief. "Alexander would never hurt anyone."

"Alcohol can change even the most mild-mannered person, my lady." Regret tinged Detective Lefèvre's voice. "And we have a witness who claims that Lord Cavendish was heavily intoxicated on the night the princess was murdered."

"A witness?" Elizabeth's eyes narrowed. "And who might that be? Perhaps they were lying, trying to deflect blame from themselves."

"I'm afraid I can't reveal the witness's identity." Detective Lefèvre's expression betrayed his conflicted duty. "But Dubois is convinced of their veracity."

"Then can I at least speak with Lord Cavendish?" she pleaded. "Even for a few minutes, I promise I won't be long."

Empathy softened Detective Lefèvre's expression as he shook his head. "I'm afraid that won't be possible." He raised a hand, forestalling her protest. "Lord Cavendish has been moved to La Maison d'Arrêt de Cannes. Dubois's orders, I'm afraid."

Elizabeth's eyes widened as another rumble of thunder sounded, closer now. "The prison?" Her heart sank. Alexander, in prison – the very thought made her stomach coil with dread. She couldn't bear the thought of him languishing behind bars with hardened criminals, his good name tarnished by baseless suspicions.

And what on earth was she going to say to Aunt Beatrice?

Chapter Fifteen

THE MORNING DAWNED FRESH, the previous day's oppressive humidity swept away by the night's fierce storm. Meli slept soundly in the adjacent bed, her brow now relaxed. Exhausted from their late-night deliberations, both had finally succumbed to sleep in the early hours.

Elizabeth sighed, their discussion weighing on her mind. They had scrutinised every discovery, debating their next move. Sharing news of Alexander's transfer to the local prison would only distress Aunt Beatrice further, so they decided against it.

The image of Alexander alone in his cell gnawed at Elizabeth. Time was running out. They needed to act before the authorities cemented their case, condemning him forever.

Elizabeth rose from her bed, mindful not to wake Meli. Dressing swiftly, she slipped into a long-sleeved, powder-blue day dress with a sashed drop waist, and tiptoed into the sitting room.

Aunt Beatrice already occupied one of the armchairs, her gaze distant as she stared out the window, her concerns for Alexander etched into the lines of her face.

She turned as Elizabeth approached, offering a weary smile.

"Is everything all right, Aunt? Where's Evelyn?"

"Yes, yes ... I'm perfectly fine." Elizabeth couldn't help but notice the way Aunt Beatrice's fingers worried the lace of her handkerchief. "I've let Evelyn sleep in after that dreadful storm, keeping us awake half the night."

Crossing to her aunt's side, Elizabeth settled into the chair next to her, giving the older woman's hand a reassuring squeeze.

"I worry for him, Elizabeth. Accused of murder, his good name tarnished..." Aunt Beatrice's gaze grew haunted, the lines of concern etching deeper into her features.

Elizabeth avoided her aunt's gaze. If she knew the truth about Alexander's transfer to La Maison d'Arrêt de Cannes – she dreaded to think what it could do to her. "Why don't we take a walk in the garden? That usually lifts your spirits."

"I'm not sure, Elizabeth. All those whispers..."

"But it's still early, Aunt. I doubt most of them will even be up yet." Elizabeth could see her aunt's resolve weaken. "And the flowers are always at their best after a little rainfall," she coaxed.

"Very well." Aunt Beatrice rose, her posture stiff. "But I must warn you, I've no patience for idle chatter today."

Elizabeth suppressed a chuckle. Her aunt had never been one to suffer fools gladly. "I'll get your shawl. The sunshine can be quite deceptive at this time of the morning. We don't want you catching a chill."

Exiting their suite, they moved down the staircase, their footsteps echoing lightly in the silence. Crossing the foyer, they observed the staff, already bustling to prepare Le Majestique for the day ahead.

Stepping outside, Aunt Beatrice inhaled deeply. The fresh air carried the damp, earthy scent of the flower beds and the sweet fragrance of blooms.

Elizabeth linked her arm through her aunt's as they navigated the pathways, pausing occasionally for Aunt Beatrice to smell the roses, the droplets of rain glistening in their folds like tiny crystals. "I must confess, I've missed my daily walks around the garden, but I couldn't abide the thought of all the gossips tittle-tattling behind my back."

Aunt Beatrice cast Elizabeth a sidelong glance. "My dear Josephine, Alexander's mother, must be turning in her grave. I promised her I'd look after Alexander as if he were my own. And to think I was encouraging him to pursue the ... that woman, when she was nothing but a criminal."

Elizabeth squeezed her aunt's arm. "You mustn't blame yourself. We were all taken in by her."

As Elizabeth and Aunt Beatrice strolled along the garden paths, they rounded a bend and came upon the familiar figure of Mr Gray. "Lady

Hawthorne, Lady Elizabeth," he greeted them, a warm smile spreading across his ruggedly handsome face. "What a delightful surprise to see you here."

His gaze settled on Aunt Beatrice. "And Lady Hawthorne, it's wonderful to see you venturing from the confines of your suite. The garden must be a welcome respite on such a lovely day."

Aunt Beatrice inclined her head, the light catching on the delicate silver tones of her chignon. "Good morning, Mr Gray. Yes, the fresh air has been most restorative."

"I'm glad to hear it." His smile widened, revealing a flash of white teeth. "I have just been for a stroll ... to buy the morning paper." Elizabeth's gaze drifted to his empty hands, noting the absence of any such publication. "I hope our backgammon game is still on this afternoon's agenda?"

Aunt Beatrice managed a faint smile. "Indeed, Mr Gray. It has become a most welcome distraction in these trying times."

"Excellent." His gaze flickered to Elizabeth, his expression unreadable, before returning to

Aunt Beatrice. "Excellent ... well, I shall leave you both to enjoy the garden."

Elizabeth watched as he hesitated, as if waiting for them to depart first, but this particular part of the garden featured some of her aunt's favourite roses - their vibrant hues and robust fragrance drawing Aunt Beatrice's attention. She tended to linger here, savouring the fleeting beauty.

Finally, he nodded and continued on his way.

Most odd, Elizabeth mused while her aunt admired the blooms.A glint caught Elizabeth's eye as Aunt Beatrice admired the blooms. Bending down, she parted the foliage and plucked a sparkling object from the wet soil—an earring, its gemstones winking in the morning light. Then she spotted something else, half-buried nearby. Elizabeth passed the earring to her aunt and knelt, fingers already reaching for the partially exposed item.

Elizabeth snatched a stick propping up a nearby plant and began to dig.

"Elizabeth!" Aunt Beatrice hissed, glancing around. "This is most unbecoming. Summon a gardener."

"One moment, Aunt." Elizabeth's fingers carefully worked the earth. "The rain's uncovered something."

She gently freed a square object, revealing a marble ashtray — identical to those at Le Majestique. Elizabeth resisted the urge to clean it, knowing it might hold crucial evidence.

Elizabeth held out her gloved hand. "May I see that earring again?"

She examined it closely, the waterfall design unmistakable despite the grime. Her eyes widened. "I'm sure this is from the pair the princess was wearing on the night of the ... opera."

Aunt Beatrice peered down, her brow creasing. "Now that you mention it, it does look rather familiar. But how on earth did it end up in the flower bed? And who would bury an ashtray there?"

"Someone who didn't want it to be found, I'd imagine." Like perhaps the murderer. Elizabeth's gaze swept the garden. "It could be a coincidence, but I think we should call the police."

"Not that odious Chief Inspector Dubois." Aunt Beatrice tutted and rolled her eyes, the disapproval clear in her expression.

Elizabeth inclined her head in agreement. "You're right, Aunt. Far better I deal with Detective Lefèvre directly." She turned to her aunt. "Would you mind staying here while I telephone the police station? I don't want anyone to disturb any evidence that could help Alexander."

Aunt Beatrice's shoulders sagged with a weary sigh. "Very well, but don't dawdle. I'd rather not be standing out here when the guests filter down for breakfast. We've already given them enough to gossip about as it is."

Elizabeth's head dipped in a firm, decisive nod. "I'll be as quick as I can."

Determined, she navigated the foyer, her pace quickening. Reaching the reception desk, she caught the receptionist's eye. The dark-haired woman straightened, surprise flickering across her face. "Is everything all right, Lady Elizabeth? You seem a little ... flustered."

Elizabeth maintained a calm demeanour. "Yes, everything is perfectly fine. There's a private matter I wish to discuss with Detective

Lefèvre. Would you be so kind as to place a telephone call to the police station?"

The receptionist's brow furrowed as she reached for the telephone. Her fingers flew over the dial. "Would you prefer to take the call somewhere more private, Lady Hawthorne?"

"That would be most appreciated." Elizabeth's gaze swept the foyer. "The alcove over there, if you don't mind."

With a discreet nod, the receptionist gestured towards the secluded nook. "Of course, Lady Elizabeth. I'll ensure you have complete privacy."

As Elizabeth stepped into the alcove, she lifted the receiver, flicking a glance towards the receptionist to confirm she'd disconnected the line. "Detective Lefèvre, this is Lady Elizabeth. You need to come to Le Majestique immediately. I'm almost certain I've—"

A faint click on the line made her freeze, her pulse quickening. Was someone listening in on her call?

Elizabeth stole a quick look back towards the reception desk, but the young woman appeared focused on her paperwork. Still, the nagging suspicion refused to subside. Where was Monsieur Róbert ?

Schooling her features, Elizabeth returned her attention to the call, her tone more measured. "Detective, I have something very important to share with you."

Detective Lefèvre's response was immediate. "I'll be right there."

Elizabeth replaced the receiver, her gaze sweeping the foyer once more. The receptionist remained at her post, but there was no sign of Monsieur Róbert.

Keen to get back to Aunt Beatrice, she turned and almost collided with Mrs Hicks.

"Oh, pardon me, Lady Elizabeth." Mrs Hicks placed a hand to her chest, her eyes widening with mild surprise. "I didn't see you there."

Elizabeth offered a warm smile, straightening her bobbed hair. "Not to worry, Mrs Hicks. It was my fault. I was somewhat preoccupied." Her gaze swept the area, searching for any sign of Monsieur Róbert .

"Well, no harm done." Mrs Hicks adjusted an earring, her gaze flickering over Elizabeth.

"How is Miss Hicks? Meli mentioned she missed her tennis lesson yesterday. I hope she's not unwell."

Mrs Hicks's brows knitted together as she sighed. "My poor Clara has been under the weather, especially with everything that's happened."

Elizabeth's expression softened. "Yes, the poor princess … to be struck down in her prime like that, and in such dreadful circumstances."

Mrs Hicks's eyes flickered, a fleeting shadow of unease crossing her face, before composing herself. "And what of Lord Cavendish's arrest and these absurd accusations against him?" She tutted in disapproval. "Anyone with eyes can see he's innocent."

Elizabeth noticed how Mrs Hicks completely overlooked her mention of the princess, honing in on Alexander's situation instead. A flicker of suspicion ignited within her.

"It's most troubling," Elizabeth began, choosing her words carefully, "Inspector Dubois is quite convinced that Alexander is the murderer. He's not even looking for any other suspects and has already moved him to La Maison d'Arrêt de Cannes."

Mrs Hicks's fingers tightened around her handbag, a tremor passing through her lips. Elizabeth continued, "But please, don't mention this to Aunt Beatrice. The whole business upsets her terribly."

Mrs Hicks turned pale, her eyes widening before she quickly gathered herself. "Of course." She managed a strained smile. "Now, if you'll excuse me, I must get back to Clara."

Elizabeth watched her leave, her mind racing. How could Mrs Hicks be so certain of Alexander's innocence unless she knew the identity of the actual murderer? Her protectiveness over Clara was well known, and it was apparent that Alexander and Clara had formed an attachment.

But would she go as far as to commit murder for her?

Or perhaps risk everything to shield her?

Chapter Sixteen

E LIZABETH'S FINGERS DRUMMED A restless rhythm against her skirt as she paced before the flower bed, eyes scanning the garden for any sign of Detective Lefèvre. Aunt Beatrice had retreated to their suite, leaving Elizabeth to stand vigil over the damning evidence.

With each passing minute, Elizabeth's unease mounted. Polite greetings and inquiries from the stirring guests fell on deaf ears as she traversed the garden path, her mind consumed by the gravity of their discovery. Where was the detective? Surely, he recognised the urgency of the situation.

Pausing, Elizabeth peered down at the earring and ashtray nestled in the damp soil. These innocuous objects could hold the key to unravelling the princess's murder – and vindicate Alexander. Her fingers curled into her palms, nails biting into the delicate skin. Time was slipping through her fingers. She couldn't afford any further delays, not with Alexander incarcerated in the notorious jail.

The crunch of gravel underfoot drew Elizabeth's attention, and she whirled around, relief washing over her as Detective Lefèvre strode into view, one of his men trailing behind him. "Detective," she called, the words rushing out, "thank goodness you're here."

Detective Lefèvre's brow furrowed, his gaze sweeping the garden before settling on the evidence. "Lady Elizabeth." He gave a curt nod, his movements brisk and efficient as he knelt to examine the items. "My apologies for the delay. I came as soon as I could."

Elizabeth's shoulders sagged slightly, the tension ebbing from her. "What do you make of it, Detective?" she asked, her words tinged with a newfound urgency.

Detective Lefèvre examined the earring and ashtray, his gloved fingers handling the evidence with great care. His brow furrowed in concentration as he scrutinised each item.

"The earring is a match to the one the princess was wearing," Detective Lefèvre stated matter-of-factly. He turned the ashtray over in his hands, nodding grimly. "See this?" He pointed to a stain on the ivory surface. "Marble is very porous - this discolouration could be blood."

Straightening, he gestured to his officer. "Have these taken back to the station for further analysis." The officer bagged the evidence and hurried off, leaving Detective Lefèvre and Elizabeth alone in the garden.

Elizabeth's gaze sharpened as she watched the meticulous gathering of evidence. "Detective, I don't believe the princess was murdered inside her suite."

Detective Lefèvre's brow arched, a hint of scepticism in his gaze. "And where exactly do you think the murder took place?"

"I believe she was murdered outside on the balcony, and if you'll accompany me to the princess's suite, I believe I can show you the evidence that supports my theory," Elizabeth said.

Detective Lefèvre considered her for a moment, then nodded. "Lead the way, Lady Elizabeth. I'm listening."

Elizabeth led the way through the hotel, feeling the weight of Monsieur Marchand's gaze on her as she crossed the foyer towards the lift, followed closely by Detective Lefèvre. As they approached the door to the princess's suite, Elizabeth paused, her hand hovering over the handle.

Elizabeth drew in a steadying breath as she crossed the threshold of the princess's suite, the oppressive weight of memory pressing down on her. Despite the room's restored order, the ghosts of her earlier discovery lingered - the crimson stain seeping into the fibres of the rug, the acrid stench of blood that had permeated the air. Even now, she could almost feel the cloying sensation of it coating her nostrils. The image of the princess's lifeless body seared into her mind.

Steeling herself, she dragged her gaze away from the empty space where the rug had once been and made her way to the French doors leading out to the balcony. This was where she needed to focus, where she might find the answers that could identify the actual murderer and free Alexander.

"Look here, Detective," she said, her voice taut with urgency as she pointed to the balcony railing. "Do you see that faint discolouration? I believe it's blood."

Detective Lefèvre followed, his brow furrowed in concentration as he examined the railing. "Hmm, it's possible." He straightened, his gaze sweeping the balcony. "But I can't see any other blood spots."

"That could be because of the rain. It could easily have washed it away," Elizabeth countered, her eyes darting around the area, determined to find something that could stop Detective Lefèvre from dismissing her theory out of hand. "Because of this." She pointed to the overhang of the balcony above and the thick ivy clinging to the wall between the princess's suite and the one next door. "Given the direction of the wind, I believe the partial coverage above and to the side shielded this area from the rain."

Detective Lefèvre exhaled slowly, rubbing the back of his neck with his hand. "I suppose it's possible, but..."

Elizabeth could sense his cynicism, but she was determined. Pointing to the loosened joints of the wooden trellis that crawled with bougainvillea vines, she continued, "And what about this? It would have been the perfect way for the killer to access the balcony without being seen by anyone inside the hotel." She shuddered, the memory of the princess's lifeless form flashing through her mind once more. "I think the murderer used the vines and trellis to scale the wall, then lay in wait out here on the balcony for the princess. In the struggle, the earring must have come loose. Then the murderer must have struck her over the head with the ashtray before dropping it over the side into the flower beds below. Then the killer moved the body inside and staged the room to look like a crime scene."

Detective Lefèvre's expression was pensive as he considered her words, his gaze searching her face. "You seem to have given this a great deal of thought, Lady Elizabeth." His eyes narrowed slightly. "Tell me, when exactly did you have the opportunity to examine the crime scene in such detail?"

Elizabeth felt a flush of unease creep up her neck, torn between the desire to be honest and the fear of Detective Lefèvre's potential reaction. Before she could respond, Meli's arrival drew the detective's attention, her dark curls dishevelled and her cheeks flushed. "Elizabeth! I've been looking everywhere for you." She turned to the detective, a shy smile on her lips. "Detective."

"*Bonjour, Mademoiselle* Diomaros," Detective Lefèvre replied, his gaze lingering on Meli with a subtle softness that did not go unnoticed by Elizabeth.

Elizabeth cast a sidelong glance at Detective Lefèvre, sensing a moment to gather her thoughts while she pondered whether to confide what she'd learned about the princess being an imposter.

Taking a steadying breath, Elizabeth steeled her nerves. "Detective, there's something else you need to know." Her fingers drummed a restless rhythm against the fabric of her skirt, betraying the unease that simmered beneath her outward composure. "We've discovered that the princess... She wasn't who she claimed to be."

Detective Lefèvre's expression remained unreadable as he studied them both for several seconds, his piercing gaze weighing each word before he spoke. "I see. I must ask, how did you come by this information?"

Elizabeth exchanged a cautious glance with Meli, deliberating the risks of revealing the full extent of their investigation. Detective Lefèvre's quiet intensity made her wary, but there was an underlying empathy in his demeanour that hinted he might not be the adversary they had thought.

"I discovered a wig—" Elizabeth began.

"A wig?" Confusion flickered across the detective's face.

"Yes," Meli continued. "It was snagged at the back of one of the drawers. We traced it back to the wig maker, who gave us the princess's *caisse postale* number, which eventually led us to the princess's apartment."

Detective Lefèvre let out a low whistle, his gaze flickering from Elizabeth to Meli. "I'm impressed. It seems Chief Inspector Dubois underestimated your investigative skills and your determination to clear your cousin's name."

Elizabeth felt a pang of regret, realising they had now shared sensitive information that could jeopardise their own investigation. "And speaking of the Chief Inspector, I suppose you'll be sharing everything I've told you with him?"

"Eventually. But the chief inspector is giving evidence at a murder trial in Marseilles for the next few days and has left instructions he's not to be disturbed..." He trailed off, a conspiratorial glint in his eyes. "Tell me, I'm assuming you've already visited the apartment?"

Elizabeth and Meli both nodded. "Of course you did," he muttered, his lips pursing into a tight line. "And what did you discover?"

Elizabeth took a breath. "We found a workshop for making counterfeit copies of jewellery, various identification papers, and documents. But when we arrived, the front door was open and someone was already inside the apartment, but it wasn't a burglar - they appeared to be searching for something else."

Detective Lefèvre furrowed his brow. "What makes you think it wasn't a burglar?"

Meli folded her arms, her voice resolute. "Because a burglar wouldn't have left behind a diamond necklace."

Detective Lefèvre tapped his chin thoughtfully. "True ... and this intruder, what did he do when he saw you?"

Elizabeth's eyes narrowed slightly. "He escaped through the window."

"Did you get a look at him?"

"Unfortunately not, but he was wearing a rather distinctive ring on his pinky finger," Elizabeth added.

Detective Lefèvre's curiosity was piqued. "Could you describe it?"

Elizabeth's expression steadied. "Most certainly ... but that's not all. We think we know what he was looking for."

Meli leaned in. "A painting. But don't worry, we've hidden it somewhere safe."

"What you've uncovered about the princess is not entirely unexpected," Detective Lefèvre said, letting out a heavy sigh. "Can I trust that what I'm about to tell you goes no further?"

Elizabeth and Meli both nodded, their expressions serious.

Detective Lefèvre sighed, his expression heavy with the weight of what he was about to reveal. "You already know she wasn't who she claimed to be. Her real name was Doreen Voss, although she also went by Rene Voss. She came from Chicago and built quite the reputation as a swindler."

He paused, his eyes moving from Elizabeth to Meli. "Madame Voss had quite the talent. She'd charm wealthy men, vanish with their fortunes, and leave devastation in her wake. Her last victim couldn't bear the humiliation of losing everything. He took his own life."

Elizabeth inhaled sharply, her eyes widening. Beside her, Meli's hand flew to her mouth.

"How dreadful." Elizabeth's fingers clenched around her handbag, her knuckles whitening.

His expression hardened. "His brother, Monsieur Spencer Roland, is a prominent businessman. He has been relentless, spending a fortune on private detectives on both sides of the

Atlantic to track her down and bring her to justice." He shook his head. "It seems she managed to stay one step ahead until now."

"Forgive me for asking, but how do you know all of this?" Elizabeth's curiosity was palpable.

Detective Lefèvre folded his arms, leaning back slightly. "I'm part of a team based in Paris. We've been on MadameVoss's trail for almost two years. She'd been swindling her way across the Riviera, always disappearing before we could gather enough evidence to arrest her."

He sighed, frustration etching lines across his forehead. "But working with Monsieur Roland and detectives from both America and France, we were finally closing in on her before ... her murder."

"And does the chief inspector know all this?" Meli's brows knitted together in puzzlement.

Detective Lefèvre shook his head. "No, it was top secret. Dubois thinks I'm here to gain experience."

Meli's hands clenched at her sides. "But surely, if he'd known all about Doreen Voss and her schemes, he would have conducted a proper investigation. Alexander wouldn't be languishing in jail for a crime he didn't commit."

"Perhaps," Detective Lefèvre conceded, rubbing his jaw. "But we couldn't risk it. Dubois might have jeopardised the entire operation. Years of work would have been for nothing."

Elizabeth could see his point, but his words still soured her mood. "Given what you've just shared and the chief inspector's absence, we need to revisit everyone's statements and alibis. Anything overlooked the first time might be crucial now." Her hazel eyes bore into him, expectant.

Detective Lefèvre glanced away, staring at a fixed point on the floor. "That could be tricky, Lady Elizabeth."

Elizabeth's tone held a sharp edge. "Come now, Detective. I've shared everything from our investigation with you. The least you can do is let me review the statements and the coroner's report."

Detective Lefèvre shifted uncomfortably, his gaze still averted. "You misunderstood, Lady Elizabeth. It's not that I'm unwilling to give you access to this information. After all, you have proved yourself to be an excellent detective."

Elizabeth's fingers drummed against her skirt, betraying her growing impatience. "Then I don't see the problem, Detective."

Letting out a heavy sigh, Detective Lefèvre finally met her gaze. "The problem is, we didn't take any statements. Dubois was convinced of Lord Cavendish's guilt and with the Mayor pressuring him to make a quick arrest, he didn't see the point in wasting time or resources on these things."

Meli's eyes widened in disbelief. "You mean to say there are no statements or reports for us to review? How can that be?"

Detective Lefèvre's expression was one of resignation. "He was convinced of Lord Cavendish's guilt from the start. The Mayor wanted a swift arrest, and Dubois obliged."

Elizabeth felt a surge of frustration. "So the entire case has been mishandled from the beginning?" Her foot tapped against the floor, betraying her growing impatience.

Her frustration simmered, her chest tightening as a flush crept up her cheeks. Realising Alexander's fate hung on a botched investigation was maddening, but frustration alone wouldn't set him free or reveal the true murderer.

Detective Lefèvre's gaze met hers. "I agree, Lady Elizabeth. We'll start by interviewing everyone at the hotel. I'll send for extra staff to assist immediately."

Elizabeth straightened, her earlier frustration giving way to resolve. With her and Detective Lefèvre leading the investigation, justice for Alexander and the late Doreen Voss was finally within reach.

Chapter Seventeen

D ETECTIVE LEFÈVRE AND ELIZABETH sat side by side in the second-floor room Monsieur Marchand had allocated for their interviews. Meli perched in the corner, her pen poised over her notebook, ready to capture every detail.

Monsieur Marchand lingered in the doorway, his fingers fiddling with his cufflinks in a nervous tic that betrayed his veneer of nonchalance. "I trust this room meets your needs, Detective?" His gaze flitted between them, transparent curiosity shining through his veneer of courtesy. "Might I inquire about your ... persons of interest?"

Detective Lefèvre's lips tightened into a polite yet guarded smile as he shared a pointed look with Elizabeth. Her delicate brow arched subtly, reinforcing the need for discretion.

"We appreciate your cooperation, Monsieur Marchand," Elizabeth intoned, her honeyed tone belying an underlying firmness. "Rest assured, we'll inform you of any pertinent developments."

Marchand's shoulders slumped, but he nodded and retreated, throwing one last lingering glance over his shoulder as the door clicked shut. Detective Lefèvre exhaled, raking a hand through his dark hair.

"Well then," he murmured, the weight of their task evident in his voice, "shall we begin?"

Elizabeth settled into her chair. "Indeed. Our suspects won't interview themselves."

Monsieur Jacques Renault breezed into the makeshift interview room, his confident stride and warm, brown eyes immediately finding Lady Elizabeth. He offered her a charming smile.

"Good morning, Lady Elizabeth. It's a pleasure to see you again." His gaze then shifted to Meli, and his smile widened. "And Mademoiselle Diomaros, how are you enjoying the delights of Cannes?"

Meli's lips quirked downward, betraying her disappointment. "I've had little opportunity for sightseeing, what with everything going on."

Detective Lefèvre cleared his throat, his tone more reserved than usual. "Monsieur Renault, thank you for joining us. We appreciate you taking the time to assist our investigation."

Renault inclined his head before settling into the chair, one ankle casually crossed over the other. "I'm happy to provide any information that may be of use. How may I be of service?"

Detective Lefèvre's piercing gaze studied the jeweller, his body language more guarded compared to Renault's open demeanour. "What brings you to Cannes, Monsieur Renault?"

"A little business, a little pleasure," Renault shrugged, his cultured voice betraying a hint of nonchalance.

Detective Lefèvre's brow furrowed. "I'm afraid I'll need you to be more specific."

Renault nodded, the light catching the subtle highlights in his neatly styled hair. "Very well. I'm here to meet a private client to facilitate the sale of some rather rare pieces."

"I'd like the name of your client," Detective Lefèvre enquired, his tone unwavering.

"Discretion is paramount in my line of work, as I'm sure you can appreciate," Renault replied, punctuating his words with a subtle, graceful gesture.

Detective Lefèvre's expression hardened. "And this is a murder investigation, Monsieur Renault, as I'm sure you can appreciate."

Renault's jaw tightened, but he relented, providing the name of his client. "But can I be assured of your ... delicacy in your dealings with him?"

Detective Lefèvre's jaw tightened. "I'll try, but I can't make any promises given the gravity of our investigation."

Elizabeth leaned forward, her curiosity palpable. "And what of the princess? Were you acquainted with her at all?"

Renault's shoulders lifted in a casual shrug. "Barely. We exchanged pleasantries, nothing more."

"And your whereabouts between midnight and four on the day of the princess's murder?" Detective Lefèvre pressed.

A wry smile played on Renault's lips. "With a lady friend. I'd prefer to keep her name private."

Detective Lefèvre's steady gaze bore into Renault, one eyebrow arching skyward.

Renault's nostrils flared as he grudgingly revealed his companion's identity.

"We'll need to confirm this," Detective Lefèvre said, his tone brooking no argument.

Renault's hand sliced the air, his irritation crackling.

Elizabeth's eyes roved over Renault's features, searching. "And Lord Cavendish? What's your connection to him?"

Surprise flickered across Renault's face before his composure snapped back into place. "Connection? There isn't one. I met him for the first time this week … you yourself introduced us, Lady Elizabeth."

"That's odd." Elizabeth leaned forward slightly, her eyes never leaving Renault's face. "My cousin shared quite a different account of your acquaintance." Her choice to say *cousin* rather than *Lord Cavendish* was calculated, emphasising their familial connection.

Renault's lips pressed into a thin line. His fingers drummed once on the armrest. "That is a surprise, since he was so insistent on secrecy. I offered to meet him in London, but he insisted on St Tropez, to ensure no one recognised him or the parure."

Elizabeth's chest tightened at the thought of Alexander's financial troubles. "I know the set well. Those emeralds are breathtaking. I'm sure securing a buyer posed no challenge?"

Renault dipped his chin, a ghost of a smile playing on his lips. "Flawless, indeed. But you understand, Lady Elizabeth, the buyer's identity must remain confidential."

"Naturally." Elizabeth inclined her head, mirroring his gesture.

Detective Lefèvre cleared his throat. "That concludes our questions for now, Monsieur Renault. We'll verify your alibi. In the meantime, you're to remain in Cannes."

Renault rose, smoothing his jacket. "At your service, Detective." He turned, flashing a dazzling smile at Elizabeth. "Lady Elizabeth, a pleasure, as always." His gaze slid to Meli, eyes twinkling. "Mademoiselle Diomaros, I hope our paths cross again soon."

Detective Lefèvre's jaw clenched, his eyes hardening at Renault's blatant charm offensive.

The door clicked shut behind Renault. Detective Lefèvre pivoted, his keen gaze darting between Elizabeth and Meli. "Your thoughts? Could Renault be entangled in the princess's murder?"

Elizabeth's brow furrowed as she mulled over Renault's performance. "His charm is undeniable, and he certainly seems to have a way with the ladies, but I'm not convinced he has an obvious motive."

Meli nodded in agreement. "True. And from what we've uncovered, his connection to the princess seems tenuous at best."

Detective Lefèvre's eyes narrowed, weighing their insights. "If his alibi holds water, I don't believe we can consider him a prime suspect at this stage." His gaze shifted to Elizabeth, a glimmer of admiration in his eyes. "That ploy with your cousin was rather clever, Lady Elizabeth."

She met the detective's gaze, her voice tinged with curiosity. "Was I that transparent?"

A hint of a smile tugged at Detective Lefèvre's lips. "To the untrained eye, perhaps not. But I caught that subtle shift – a flicker of confidence that betrayed your gambit."

A soft chuckle escaped Elizabeth's lips, her shoulders relaxing. "I'll have to polish my poker face, it seems."

Detective Lefèvre's eyes crinkled with amusement. He straightened, all business once more. "Shall we proceed to our next person of interest?"

Minutes later, the door swung open, heralding Monsieur Gray's arrival. His salt-and-pepper hair gleamed under the room's harsh light, each strand perfectly in place. Gray's eyes swept the room, a practiced smile on his lips.

Detective Lefèvre leaned forward, his elbows resting on the table. "Monsieur Gray, thank you for joining us."

Gray sank into the chair, his posture relaxed yet alert. "Happy to oblige. How can I be of assistance?"

"We're investigating Princess Sofia de' Medici's death," Detective Lefèvre's gaze bore into Gray. "Where were you between midnight and four on the night in question?"

"I was in the hotel bar?"

Elizabeth's eyebrows arched. "Until four?"

"Unfortunately so." Gray's eyes tightened at the corners, a fleeting shadow of exhaustion crossing his face. "Insomnia's my constant companion, I'm afraid."

Detective Lefèvre's eyes narrowed, his fingers steepled beneath his chin. "Any witnesses?"

"The barman, and I believe Monsieur Róbert was on duty."

Elizabeth's mind raced, recalling the assistant manager's swift arrival that fateful night.

She leaned in, her eyes never leaving Gray's face. "How well did you know the princess, Mr Gray?"

"Barely at all." Gray's tone remained smooth, unruffled. "Our opera excursion was our first real interaction."

A knowing smile played on Elizabeth's lips. "Curious, then, that you knew her preferred cocktail - a Champs-Élysées with Meyer lemon. It's rather obscure, wouldn't you say?"

Gray's composure faltered for a heartbeat before snapping back into place. "Precisely why it caught my attention. I overheard the order at the bar one evening and turned to see who'd made such an intriguing choice."

Detective Lefèvre's eyes narrowed. "What brings you to Cannes, Monsieur Gray?"

Gray reclined, his posture a study in affected ease. "I've always wanted to travel, and now that I've retired, I thought it was the perfect opportunity."

"Travelling solo?" Detective Lefèvre's tone sharpened.

"Indeed." Gray's jaw tightened. "Is solitude a crime now, Detective?"

"No … no, of course not." Detective Lefèvre's shoulders tensed, his gaze sharpening as he studied Gray's face.

Elizabeth leaned in, her voice a blend of curiosity and charm. "Are you married?"

A shadow flitted across Gray's features. "Wedded to my work, I'm afraid. My wife … she took the children and left."

"And your line of work?" Detective Lefèvre pressed.

Gray's hesitation was fleeting. "A little of everything, really."

"Care to elaborate?" Detective Lefèvre's gaze didn't waver.

"Sales, mostly." Gray's smile widened, a mask sliding into place. "It suits my ... particular talents."

Elizabeth's eyes danced with feigned admiration. "I can see how sales would suit you, Mr Gray."

Gray preened under her attention. "Yes, I find I have quite the knack for reading people. The key is being able to change and adapt to the situation and the client."

Elizabeth leaned closer, her interest a carefully crafted performance. "I envy that skill. I'm dreadful at reading people."

"You're too modest, Lady Elizabeth," he purred. "It's all in the details – family photos, hobby hints. Steer the conversation there, claim a shared passion. Soon, they're putty in your hands."

"You make it sound effortless," Elizabeth breathed, seemingly captivated.

His chest puffed slightly. "Like all things worth mastering, Lady Elizabeth, it requires practice."

"Indeed." Elizabeth's mind raced, peeling back the layers of Southern charm to reveal the calculating operator beneath.

Mr Gray's eyes flicked to the clock. "Do you have any other questions for me? I have a very important appointment this afternoon, one that calls into question my very honour." His face became unusually serious for a moment before a chuckle escaped his lips. "My backgammon match with a most formidable opponent."

Detective Lefèvre's gaze bore into Gray. "That's all for now. We'll need to verify your alibi with the barman and Monsieur Róbert, but in the meantime, you're to remain in Cannes."

Gray rose, adjusting the cuffs of his jacket. "With such charming company and stunning vistas, staying put will be no hardship." He paused at the door. "I hope you find your man soon, Detective ... or woman." The door clicked shut behind him.

"What an odd thing to say." Meli broke the silence. "What makes him think that the murderer is a woman?"

"It's a possibility," Elizabeth mused. "But yes, a strange comment to make ... unless he knows more than he's letting on."

She turned to Detective Lefèvre. "Your thoughts on our cryptic Mr Gray, Detective?"

Detective Lefèvre's jaw tightened. "He's concealing something, that's clear. But a murderer? I'm not convinced ... yet."

"And his parting comment?" Elizabeth pressed.

Detective Lefèvre's shoulders lifted in a slight shrug. "Could be deflection. Gray warrants further scrutiny. I'll contact some of my colleagues in Paris and see if they've come across him before."

Meli snorted. "I don't trust him an inch. If he wasn't so hopeless at backgammon, I doubt Aunt Beatrice would tolerate him."

Elizabeth's eyes narrowed, recalling Gray's earlier boast about excellence through practice. The contradiction gnawed at her. "Mr Gray is indeed an enigma. I concur, Detective. We need to delve deeper."

Detective Lefèvre nodded. "In the meantime, I'll have one of my men follow him."

Following Mr Gray's departure, Monsieur Bouchér swept into the room, a dark fedora perched atop his head, a single iridescent peacock feather curling elegantly from the hatband. With a dismissive flick of his wrist, he removed the hat and set it on the table, his gaze coolly appraising the detectives.

"Monsieur Bouchér, thank you for joining us." Detective Lefèvre's tone was clipped, betraying little interest in pleasantries. "I understand you have a busy schedule, so let's get straight to it. What brings you to Cannes?"

Bouchér's lips thinned into a tight-lipped frown. "If we must." He leaned back in his chair, the picture of reluctant cooperation. "I'm the organiser of the art auction that was held at this hotel."

Detective Lefèvre's brow lifted. "And do you often find yourself in Cannes for such events?"

"When the need arises." Monsieur Bouchér's response was curt, his body language radiating impatience.

Sensing Monsieur Bouchér's waning patience, Elizabeth jumped in. "Are you acquainted with Princess Sofia?"

Bouchér's head shook in a curt denial. "No, I've never met her before."

"Not even in passing? Perhaps in the bar or lounge?"

Bouchér's shoulders rose in a long-suffering sigh. "I suppose I could have exchanged a brief greeting, but I know so many people in the art world. I can't be expected to remember everyone." His gaze flicked to the clock. "Is this going to take long?"

Elizabeth exchanged a pointed look with Detective Lefèvre.

The detective's eyes narrowed, his voice hardening. "Do you have an alibi for the time of the princess's murder?"

Bouchér drew a steadying breath, his composure slipping. "I was delivering a painting to a client."

Elizabeth found it curious that Monsieur Bouchér , a prominent art broker, would take on such a menial task.

Detective Lefèvre leaned forward. "You drove through the night?"

"It was a long drive." Monsieur Bouchér's gaze darted to the ornate clock on the mantelpiece, then back to Lefèvre.

Elizabeth's eyes narrowed as she studied him. "Can you provide the name of the client?"

Bouchér's eyes flickered with anxiety. "I must protect the privacy of my clients."

Detective Lefèvre's demeanour turned stern. "This is a murder investigation, Monsieur Bouchér."

Bouchér's shoulders slumped, his nervousness now palpable. "The client wasn't home when I arrived, so they can't confirm my alibi."

Detective Lefèvre's brow furrowed. "Was there anyone who might have seen you during this time?"

Bouchér's beady eyes darted around the room, sweat beading on his brow. "No," he replied, his voice wavering.

Sensing a need for a break to further pressure Monsieur Bouchér, Detective Lefèvre rose. "Thank you, Monsieur Bouchér. I think this is an excellent place to take a brief break."

Elizabeth, Detective Lefèvre, and Meli excused themselves, Detective Lefèvre's gaze hardening as he instructed the policeman. "Make sure Monsieur Bouchér doesn't leave."

While Elizabeth and Meli retreated to the hotel lounge, Detective Lefèvre took the opportunity to confer with his officers. The detectives had spent the day interviewing the hotel staff, and Detective Lefèvre was eager to hear their findings.

Sipping her coffee, Meli's eyes twinkled with mischief. "So, what do you make of Detective Lefèvre?"

Elizabeth feigned nonchalance. "He seems a capable investigator."

Meli's pout betrayed her dissatisfaction. "That's not what I meant, and you know it."

Elizabeth chuckled, relenting. "He's a perfectly pleasant young man."

"Do you think he's handsome?" Meli leaned in, her curiosity palpable.

Elizabeth's shoulders lifted in a dismissive shrug. "I suppose so, but he's not my type."

Meli's eyes gleamed. "And who is more your type? A certain Mr Jonathan Ashcroft, perhaps?"

A flush crept up Elizabeth's neck, but she brushed off Meli's teasing. "I barely know him."

Meli grinned. "That's not what Clemmi Mayfield says. She insists Mr Ashcroft is quite taken with you."

Elizabeth felt a flutter of pleasure, quickly smothered by a wave of irritation. Jonathan Ashcroft. Even his name stirred a whirlwind of conflicting emotions within her.

She pictured his face: those piercing green eyes that seemed to see right through her, the hint of a roguish smile that both charmed and infuriated her. He was undeniably handsome, but it was more than that. There was a depth to him, a complexity that both intrigued and unsettled her.

Elizabeth's brow furrowed as she recalled their encounters. Twice now, he had put himself in harm's way to protect her. The memory of his quick thinking and decisive actions in those moments of danger sent an involuntary shiver down her spine. Such selfless acts spoke volumes about his character, yet...

She couldn't shake the nagging doubt that clouded her judgment. Jonathan Ashcroft was an enigma, his motives often unclear. One moment, he was the picture of a perfect gentleman, the next, he was infuriatingly evasive.

She sighed, frustrated by her own indecision. Part of her longed to unravel the mystery that was Jonathan Ashcroft, while another part warned her to keep her distance. It was a predicament that both excited and exasperated her, much like the man himself.

Detective Lefèvre entered the lounge, his sudden appearance startling Elizabeth from her thoughts.

"Ready to resume?" He tapped his watch. "Bouchér's had enough time to sweat."

Meli sprang up, her enthusiasm palpable. "Absolutely!"

The lift doors slid open on the second floor, revealing an unsettling quiet. As they approached the interview room, Elizabeth's skin prickled. The door stood ajar, defying Detective Lefèvre's explicit instructions.

The guard hovered nearby, his cap clutched in trembling hands, face drained of colour.

Detective Lefèvre's footsteps faltered. "Explain. Now."

"I heard–" The guard's voice cracked. He swallowed hard. "A noise, sir. I checked, and–"

Elizabeth shouldered past them, shoving the door wide. Papers littered the floor like fallen leaves, furniture lay toppled. The open window beckoned, curtains dancing in the breeze.

She lunged for the sill, gripping the frame as she leaned out.

A figure bounded across the rooftops, agile as a cat. "There!"

Detective Lefèvre materialised beside her, a string of curses escaping through clenched teeth. He whirled, voice sharp. "Lock it down! Every exit!"

As chaos erupted around her, questions ricocheted through Elizabeth's mind. Watching Monsieur Bouchér make his escape triggered an odd feeling of déjà vu.

Chapter Eighteen

Monsieur Bouchér's daring escape had left them all reeling, the shock still palpable in the air. Elizabeth's mind whirled, an unsettling sense of familiarity clinging to her like a persistent fog. The image of the art broker's lithe form disappearing across the rooftops played on repeat in her mind's eye. But with Monsieur Bouchér on the run, their best lead had slipped through their fingers. Without him in custody, they had no way to extract the truth about his connection to the princess or his motives for breaking into her apartment.

The interview room door creaked open, the sound grating in the tense silence. Detective Lefèvre burst in, his usual composure fracturing under the weight of mounting pressure. His jaw clenched tight, a muscle twitching beneath his skin.

Elizabeth's gaze locked onto the detective, her spine snapping straight as a rod. "Our next move?" The words hung in the air, laden with urgency.

Detective Lefèvre prowled across the room, tension radiating from every line of his body. "We push on." His eyes darted between Elizabeth and Meli, razor-sharp and unyielding. "Dubois returns in days. Every second counts."

The chief inspector's name fell like a lead weight, thickening the already oppressive atmosphere. Elizabeth's fingers curled into tight fists, nails biting crescents into her palms. Chief Inspector Dubois and his bull-headed conviction had already squandered precious time.

Detective Lefèvre seemed to sense her frustration, his own determination mirroring hers. His eyes narrowed, voice dropping to a low, determined growl. "Time to see what Miss Hicks has to say for herself." He jerked his chin towards the door, a silent command to his officer to fetch their next interviewee.

Moments later, Clara Hicks entered, her usual poise faltering as she crossed the threshold. She took the seat opposite Detective Lefèvre, her fingers fidgeting with the fabric of her dress.

Detective Lefèvre leaned forward, his piercing gaze fixed on Clara. "Miss Hicks, what brings you to Cannes?"

Clara swallowed hard, her voice barely above a whisper. "My father passed away nine months ago. Since then, Mother and I have been ... travelling." She paused, her eyes flickering with a mix of grief and uncertainty. "I think she finds it difficult to be at home. Too many memories."

Elizabeth studied Clara, her heart clenching at the sight before her. The young woman's shoulders were taut with tension, her knuckles white as she gripped her dress. Clara's usual vibrancy had vanished, replaced by an ashen pallor and a sheen of perspiration on her brow. Her gaze darted between Detective Lefèvre and the door like a trapped animal, a fragile, haunted look in her eyes that spoke volumes of her inner turmoil. As Clara answered Detective Lefèvre's questions, her voice barely above a whisper,

Elizabeth couldn't help but feel a wave of sympathy for the distressed young woman.

Detective Lefèvre's piercing gaze bore into Clara. "Miss Hicks, where were you on the night of the princess's murder?"

Clara's chest rose with a shaky breath, her spine stiffening as if bracing for impact. "Mother and I dined at *La Rotonde* that evening." She paused, her lower lip trembling slightly. "Afterwards, we visited the casino."

Her fingers twisted in her lap, the fabric of her dress crumpling under her grip. "I'm afraid I don't recall the exact hour we left. It wasn't late. Mother was…" Clara's voice cracked, a hint of guilt flickering across her features. "She was on a winning streak and reluctant to leave, but I had a headache."

Detective Lefèvre leaned forward, his chair creaking. "Can anyone confirm your presence at these establishments?"

"The Maître d', perhaps? Or the hostess?" Clara's gaze skittered away, unable to meet the detective's probing stare.

Detective Lefèvre's jaw clenched, a muscle twitching beneath his skin. "And at the casino – did anyone witness your departure?"

Clara seemed to shrink in on herself, her shoulders hunching as if to ward off the weight of the question. "I'm not certain. There were so many people, and it was particularly busy."

Elizabeth leaned in, her voice gentle. "Clara, think carefully. Even the smallest detail could be crucial."

Clara's brow furrowed in concentration, her teeth worrying at her lower lip. "Mr Gray – the American gentleman. We left at the same time. He was in quite a state, refused Mother's offer of a ride back to the hotel."

"Why was he upset?" Detective Lefèvre demanded, his tone sharp.

Clara flinched at his tone, her fingers curling tighter into her palms. "He said he'd had some bad luck at the tables."

"And what time was this?"

"Just after midnight, I believe." Clara's voice had dwindled to nothing more than a whisper.

Detective Lefèvre's voice cut through the air like a whip. "What happened when you returned to the hotel?"

Clara's gaze dropped to her lap, her lashes damp with unshed tears. "I read for a little while before retiring for the evening."

"Are you certain you didn't leave your room again?"

At this, Clara's composure shattered. Tears spilled down her cheeks as she struggled to form words. "Lord Cavendish," she choked out, "he came to my door after Mother had gone to bed. He was so desperately unhappy, in need of someone to talk to." Her eyes, wide and pleading, sought understanding. "But nothing improper happened, I swear it. Alexander never even entered my suite."

Detective Lefèvre's expression darkened, his eyes glinting dangerously. "So you're admitting you met with Lord Cavendish that evening?"

Clara nodded, her face a mask of anguish and fear.

Detective Lefèvre leaned back, his gaze unyielding. "Can anyone corroborate your account, Miss Hicks? Or is this simply the desperate tale of a woman trying to protect the man she loves?"

Clara's fingers twisted in her lap, her knuckles white with tension. "No," she whispered, her voice thick with despair. "Alexander made sure no one saw us. He wanted to protect my reputation." She looked up, her eyes brimming with fresh tears. "You won't tell my mother, will you? She's been so protective since my father died."

Elizabeth reached across the table, grasping Clara's trembling hand. The young woman's skin felt cold and clammy beneath her touch. "I believe you, Clara," she said softly, "but you must understand. This information is crucial to proving Alexander's innocence. Without it, he could spend the rest of his life in jail."

Clara's breath hitched, her eyes wide with dawning realisation. "I... I understand," she whispered, her voice trembling. "I'll tell you everything, Detective. For Alexander's sake."

Detective Lefèvre nodded, his stern expression softening slightly. "Very well, Miss Hicks. Let's start from the beginning. Tell me exactly what happened that night."

As Clara recounted the events in detail, Elizabeth felt a mix of relief and apprehension. She knew this testimony could be pivotal in clearing Alexander's name, but she also understood the personal cost to Clara.

As Clara left the room, her shoulders slumped with exhaustion, Elizabeth felt a pang of sympathy. The door clicked shut, leaving a heavy silence in its wake.

Meli, who had been uncharacteristically quiet throughout the interview, suddenly burst out, "How could you treat her like that? She's obviously innocent!"

Detective Lefèvre's eyebrows shot up at the outburst. "Mademoiselle, I was just doing my job."

"Your job?" Meli scoffed, her eyes flashing. "Bullying a young woman like that?"

Elizabeth placed a placating hand on her cousin's arm. "Meli, please."

Detective Lefèvre sighed, rubbing his temples. "I understand your frustration, but we needed to be certain of Miss Hicks's account."

"Well, I for one believe her," Meli declared, chin lifted defiantly.

Elizabeth nodded. "I agree. Clara's not the murderer."

To their surprise, Detective Lefèvre nodded. "On that, we are in agreement."

Elizabeth straightened, a new thought occurring to her. "Speaking of accounts, Clara placed Mr Gray at the casino, yet he never mentioned it in his interview. The Hicks could have confirmed his whereabouts. Why would he omit that?"

Detective Lefèvre's eyes narrowed. "Mr Gray appears to be quite ... selective with his recollections."

Meli looked up from her notes, her pen hovering above the paper. "And his explanation for knowing the princess's cocktail preference? I don't buy it for a second."

Detective Lefèvre nodded, his fingers tapping the desk once. "We need to question Mr Gray again. These inconsistencies demand clarification."

He exhaled, squaring his shoulders. "For now, though, we focus on Miss Hicks's account. Her testimony could be crucial."

"Crucial indeed," Elizabeth leaned forward eagerly. "Surely Clara's statement gives Alexander an alibi. He should be released immediately."

Detective Lefèvre's expression darkened. "It's not that simple, Lady Elizabeth. I don't have the authority to release him."

"But if Chief Inspector Dubois—" Elizabeth began.

Detective Lefèvre cut her off with a sharp shake of his head. "Dubois won't sanction Lord Cavendish's release. He'll claim Miss Hicks only provided an alibi because she's in love with him."

Meli let out an exasperated huff. "That's preposterous!"

"Perhaps," Detective Lefèvre conceded, "but it's how Dubois will see it. And his word is final."

Elizabeth felt her heart sink. They were so close to clearing Alexander's name, yet still so far from securing his freedom. She met Meli's frustrated gaze, then turned back to Detective Lefèvre.

"So what do we do now, Detective?"

Detective Lefèvre's response was cut short by a commotion outside. The door swung open and Mrs Laura Hicks strode in, her steely gaze sweeping the space. She exuded an air of unshakeable confidence, a stark contrast to her daughter's earlier fragility.

Fixing Detective Lefèvre with a razor-sharp glare, she leaned forward. "Before we begin, Detective, let's establish some ground rules. One misstep, and my lawyers will descend on your superiors like vultures."

Detective Lefèvre's eyes narrowed. "Is that a threat, Mrs Hicks?"

"Consider it ... friendly advice." Her smile was honey-sweet, but her eyes glinted like polished flint. "I believe in transparency, Detective. Now we both know where we stand."

Elizabeth shifted in her seat, taken aback by this new side of Mrs Hicks. The pleasant, sociable woman she knew had transformed into a formidable adversary.

Detective Lefèvre's jaw tightened. "Duly noted." He wasted no time on pleasantries. "What brings you to Cannes?"

Mrs Hicks arched an eyebrow, her voice laced with derision. "My daughter and I are travelling. Is that suddenly a crime?"

"Not at all. First time here?"

For a fleeting moment, Mrs Hicks's iron façade cracked. A shadow of grief flitted across her face. "No," she murmured, her voice softening. "I've been here before ... with my late husband."

Detective Lefèvre's eyes narrowed. "Where were you between midnight and four on the night of the princess's murder?"

"Asleep in my bed," Mrs Hicks snapped. "Clara can vouch for that."

Her jaw clenched, daring Detective Lefèvre to question her further.

Undaunted, he pressed on. "Did you know the princess personally?"

Mrs Hicks's lip curled. "Not personally, no. But I recognised her type." Her eyes flashed. "Flaunting herself, chasing after every man in sight."

Detective Lefèvre leaned in. "Is that why you disliked her? Because she pursued Lord Cavendish?"

"Lord Cavendish's affairs are irrelevant to me," she retorted, ice in her voice.

"But isn't it true that you had your sights set on Lord Cavendish as a suitable match for your daughter?" Detective Lefèvre pressed, his eyes sharp.

Mrs Hicks's nostrils flared. "Clara is free to marry whomever she chooses."

Detective Lefèvre's gaze bore into her. "I'm sure you've been aware of your daughter's feelings for Lord Cavendish. And perhaps as a doting mother, you were determined to secure him for her, but the princess got in the way."

A harsh laugh escaped Mrs Hicks. "If I wanted to buy a title, Detective, I wouldn't waste time on the penniless Earl of Wexford." Her smile dripped contempt. "Clara could have her pick of Europe's finest."

Elizabeth's heart sank as Mrs Hicks parried each question, her evasions as smooth as silk.

The room fell silent as Detective Lefèvre's officer entered, handing him a folded note. His eyes flicked over the contents, a triumphant smile tugging at the corners of his mouth.

Detective Lefèvre turned to Mrs Hicks, leaning forward. "It seems we've uncovered an interesting development, madam." His voice held a hint of amusement.

Mrs Hicks's brow furrowed, her carefully maintained composure wavering.

"One of the hotel maids," Detective Lefèvre said, tapping the note, "claims to have seen you outside the princess's suite in the early hours of the morning on the day of her murder."

Mrs Hicks's face paled, her eyes widening. "That's impossible!" Her usual poise vanished. "I was in my room, asleep, as I told you!"

Detective Lefèvre shook his head. "We have a witness who says otherwise." His gaze didn't waver from hers. "What were you doing outside the princess's door at that hour, Mrs Hicks?"

Mrs Hicks's mouth opened and closed, words failing her. Elizabeth watched, transfixed, as the formidable woman's composure crumbled, her air of superiority dissolving under Detective Lefèvre's steady gaze.

Chapter Nineteen

SILENCE STRETCHED TAUT AS a bowstring in the interview room. Mrs Hicks sat rigid, her fingers digging into the chair arms, knuckles bleached white. Across from her, Detective Lefèvre leaned forward, his gaze boring into her. The detective's jaw clenched, a muscle twitching beneath his skin. Mrs Hicks's eyes darted between Detective Lefèvre and the door, reminiscent of a fox eyeing an escape route. Time stretched thin, pulled taut by the clock's unrelenting rhythm. Elizabeth shifted in her seat, the leather creaking softly, waiting for someone to finally break the silence.

Mrs Hicks's rigid posture faltered. Her shoulders sagged, the fight draining from her frame. She opened her mouth, then closed it, her lips pressed into a thin line. Her gaze dropped to her hands, now twisting in her lap. After a long moment, she lifted her chin, meeting Detective Lefèvre's unwavering stare. "Very well," she said, her voice rough with reluctance. She swallowed hard before continuing. "I left our room that night. I slipped out, taking care not to wake Clara, and made my way to the princess's suite."

Detective Lefèvre's eyes flashed, his voice sharp as a blade. "To murder her? To clear the path for your daughter and Lord Cavendish?"

Mrs Hicks recoiled, her face draining of colour before flushing crimson. Her fingers curled into fists, knuckles white against her skirt. Mrs Hicks's gaze sharpened. "Don't be so ridiculous," she hissed through grated teeth. "I might have disliked the woman, but I certainly didn't wish to see her dead."

Detective Lefèvre's fingers drummed a staccato beat on the table. His gaze never wavered from Mrs Hicks's face. "Then explain your nocturnal visit, Mrs Hicks. Why risk your reputation prowling the halls at that hour?"

Mrs Hicks's jaw clenched, her nostrils flaring. She exhaled. "I went to buy her off."

Detective Lefèvre's eyebrows shot up, his chair creaking as he leaned forward. "Elaborate."

Mrs Hicks's gaze dropped to her lap, her fingers twisting the fabric of her skirt. "That 'princess' was as transparent as glass from the moment she sashayed into Le Majestique. Flaunting her counterfeit jewels and cheap finery, latching onto any man with a hefty wallet."

Elizabeth's eyes widened, her curiosity piqued. "How could you tell they were fake?"

A bitter smile twisted Mrs Hicks's lips. Her eyes, hard as flint, met Elizabeth's. "My husband and I started with nothing. He built his fortune through grit and sweat." She paused, her voice low and intense. "I've lived on both sides of the coin. I know the difference between genuine wealth and a desperate imitation."

Detective Lefèvre leaned forward, his voice low. "And what were you demanding in exchange for this payment?"

"For her to leave Cannes." Mrs Hicks's gaze met his unflinchingly.

Detective Lefèvre's chair groaned as he shifted closer. "What happened? Did she refuse to leave, and you snapped? Grabbed the nearest object and hit her?"

Mrs Hicks jerked back. "Absolutely not!" Her voice wavered. "She wouldn't even open the door!"

"Wouldn't?" Detective Lefèvre's voice sharpened. "Not couldn't?"

Mrs Hicks's gaze darted away. "She … she was inside. I heard voices."

Detective Lefèvre's eyebrows arched. "Voices? Plural?"

Mrs Hicks nodded, her spine straightening. "A man and a woman." Her eyes locked onto Detective Lefèvre's. "And before you ask—" she raised a hand as Detective Lefèvre's mouth opened "—it wasn't Lord Cavendish. I know his voice well enough."

At Mrs Hicks's words, Elizabeth's shoulders visibly relaxed, the tension melting away. With the evidence mounting that proved Alexander's innocence, Chief Inspector Dubois would have to see sense and release him.

"What did you do then?" Detective Lefèvre pressed, his voice low and insistent.

Mrs Hicks's chin lifted a fraction. "I returned to my room, of course."

Detective Lefèvre's eyes narrowed, studying her face. His fingers drummed once, twice on the table. "And you're certain you heard two distinct voices? Male and female?"

"Yes." Mrs Hicks met his gaze unflinchingly. "I'm not in the habit of fabricating stories, Detective."

Detective Lefèvre leaned back, his chair groaning. He glanced at Elizabeth, then back to Mrs Hicks. "Did you recognise the male voice?"

Mrs Hicks's lips thinned. "No. It was muffled, but ... unfamiliar."

Silence stretched between them, taut as a wire. Detective Lefèvre's gaze never wavered from Mrs Hicks's face. Finally, he nodded. "That will be all for now, Mrs Hicks. I must ask you to remain in Cannes until further notice. We may need to speak with you again."

Mrs Hicks rose, her movements stiff. At the threshold, she paused, her hand on the doorknob. "Alexander is no more a murderer than you or I, Detective." The door clicked shut behind her, leaving a heavy silence in its wake.

Elizabeth exhaled slowly, her gaze meeting Detective Lefèvre's across the table.

Meli leaned forward, her eyes flicking between Elizabeth and the detective. "Do we believe her?"

Detective Lefèvre's fingers traced his chin, his eyes distant. "She'd certainly try to remove a perceived threat to her daughter, of that I have no doubt."

Elizabeth's brow creased. "I concur, but murder? It doesn't fit."

"No," Detective Lefèvre agreed, his gaze sharpening. "Whatever Mrs Hicks is, I don't believe she's a killer."

Elizabeth sat up straighter, a realisation dawning. "Detective, Mrs Hicks's testimony changes our timeline. If she heard the princess alive at one o'clock, and the body was already showing signs of early rigor mortis when I found her body just after six…"

Detective Lefèvre nodded, his expression grave. "Indeed. It narrows our window considerably. The murder likely occurred between one and two, not between midnight and four, as we initially thought."

Meli's eyes widened. "That's a much smaller timeframe and helps us narrow down the list of suspects?"

"I concur," Elizabeth mused.

Detective Lefèvre's lips thinned. "But it also means we need to re-evaluate all the statements we've collected so far. I'll get some of my men to work on verifying everyone's alibis."

The detective's words hung in the air, a reminder of the complex web of testimonies they'd gathered throughout the day. Elizabeth nodded, feeling the weight of each interview settling on her shoulders.

She stifled a yawn, the long day of interviews weighing heavily on her. Her mind felt foggy, struggling to piece together the disparate threads of information they'd gathered from Monsieur Renault, Mr Gray, Miss Hicks, and Mrs Hicks. The image of Monsieur Bouchér's hasty escape through the window flashed in her memory, adding to her sense of mental fatigue.

Detective Lefèvre glanced at the clock, then back at Elizabeth and Meli. "I think that's enough for today. We'll continue in the morning."

Meli's sigh of relief was audible. "Thank goodness. I've written so much, I fear my hand might detach itself in protest."

Elizabeth nodded, grateful for the reprieve. As they rose to leave, an officer appeared at the door, his expression triumphant.

"*Détective Lefèvre, nous avons appréhendé Monsieur Bouchér .*"

Detective Lefèvre's eyebrows rose. "*Excellent travail. Enfermez-le dans les cellules pour la nuit.*"

The detective turned to Elizabeth and Meli, noting their curious expressions. "Bouchér has been apprehended," he explained, switching to English. "A night in the cells might loosen his tongue."

Elizabeth's mind raced at the news of Monsieur Bouchér's capture, her earlier fatigue forgotten. Felix Bouchér, the man who'd fled rather than face questioning, clearly had something to hide. Could he be their murderer? If so, Alexander's freedom was within reach. She pushed the thought aside, wary of premature conclusions.

Meli's eyes widened. "Do you think he'll confess?"

Elizabeth met her cousin's gaze. "It's possible, but we shouldn't count on it. Monsieur Bouchér's sudden flight marked him as suspicious, but his motives remain unclear."

With a sigh, Elizabeth rose from her chair, her muscles protesting after hours of intense questioning. She glanced at Meli, who looked equally drained. Elizabeth rubbed her temples. "I think we've done all we can for today."

They exited the interview room, the day's revelations still echoing in their minds. Detective Lefèvre remained behind, his low voice carrying as he conferred with an officer in rapid French.

"Did you hear Detective Lefèvre speaking French earlier? The way he rolled his R's…" She fanned herself dramatically. "*Mon Dieu*, it made my heart flutter."

Elizabeth arched an eyebrow, unable to contain a chuckle. "Really, Meli, you're impossible."

Meli shrugged, a mischievous glint in her eye. "I'm merely making an observation, cousin. Besides, a brief distraction from murder isn't such a bad thing, is it?"

Elizabeth shook her head, a small smile tugging at her lips despite herself.

Detective Lefèvre barrelled past them, his shoulder brushing Elizabeth's as he passed. His jaw clenched, eyes fixed ahead as he descended the stairs two at a time, weaving between startled guests.

Meli tugged at Elizabeth's sleeve. "Did you see his face? Something's happened."

They hurried to the railing. Below, the reception area seethed with activity. Officers in dark uniforms prowled between clusters of guests, who pressed themselves against the walls, hands covering whispered conversations.

Detective Lefèvre stood near the centre, leaning in close to a man Elizabeth didn't recognise. His hands moved in sharp, precise gestures, his words lost in the din.

Meli's fingers tightened on the railing. "What on earth's going on? Do you think they've arrested the murderer?"

Elizabeth shook her head slightly. "I'm not sure."

The crowd parted. Monsieur Marchand appeared, an officer at each elbow. His wrists were bound, metal glinting in the chandelier light. His slicked-back hair fell across his forehead, his elegant demeanour shattered.

"*Mon Dieu!*" Meli's hand flew to her mouth, her eyes wide.

Elizabeth's gaze locked onto Marchand's retreating figure, her mind racing. A memory flashed – tailored trousers and polished shoes in the princess's suite, unmistakably Le Majestique's management livery. She'd been uncertain then if it was Monsieur Marchand or Monsieur Róbert. Now, that fleeting glimpse took a sinister turn.

As Monsieur Marchand vanished from view, a chilling question formed: had they just witnessed the princess's murderer being led away in handcuffs?

Chapter Twenty

Aunt Beatrice sat rigidly in her chair, the porcelain teacup poised in her grasp. Her silvered chignon caught the muted light, not a strand daring to stray from its impeccable arrangement. Elizabeth watched as her aunt's jaw tightened with each measured sip, the liquid barely disturbing the surface of the cup.

Since Alexander's arrest, Aunt Beatrice had sequestered herself within the confines of their suite, determined to avoid the whispers and speculation she was convinced occupied the gossips. But with the arrest of Monsieur Marchand the previous evening, Elizabeth was certain the busybodies had moved on to the latest intrigue engulfing Le Majestique.

"Aunt, might we have lunch in the dining room today? The garden terrace could offer a welcome change." Elizabeth's voice was gentle, hopeful.

Aunt Beatrice's gaze sharpened, her lips thinning. "Absolutely not. I won't subject myself or this family to idle gossip. We'll dine here, away from prying eyes."

"But Aunt," Meli interjected, reaching for a croissant, a glint in her eye, "wouldn't you'd relish the chance to share your insights on Marchand? You were right about him from the start."

"I knew he wasn't to be trusted the minute I set eyes on him." A flicker of temptation crossed Aunt Beatrice's face before she shook her head, the ostrich feather in her cap quivering. "No, I shall rise above it. Besides, Mr Gray is due for our backgammon match."

She drummed her fingers on the table. "Although Mr Gray seems to think backgammon is a talking sport. Perhaps I should introduce him to debating instead."

"Yes, he does like the sound of his own voice," Meli said, rolling her eyes.

"If he hasn't mentioned his time working at Barnum & Bailey a hundred times, he hasn't mentioned it once."

"I can quite imagine him as the ringmaster." Meli giggled, buttering a slice of toast.

Evelyn's brow creased in concentration. "I don't think he was the ringmaster. I think he was one of the acts, a juggler perhaps?"

"The man's incessant chatter is enough to drive one to distraction. He asks so many questions it makes my head spin." Aunt Beatrice sighed, her fingers drumming a sharp rhythm on the arm of her chair. "Perhaps if he'd focus on the game half as much as he does on talking, he might prove a more worthy opponent."

Elizabeth leaned forward, her interest piqued. "What sort of questions does he ask, Aunt?"

Aunt Beatrice sniffed, her chin tilting upward. "I can't recall precisely. Unlike Mr Gray, I concentrate on the game at hand."

Elizabeth caught Meli's eye, exchanging a small smile at their aunt's lack of patience with her backgammon partner.

Elizabeth straightened in her chair. "Aunt Beatrice, Meli and I need to visit the police station this morning. We have more interviews to conduct."

Aunt Beatrice nodded, her fingers smoothing the tablecloth. "Very well. I'd best prepare myself for Mr Gray's visit later. No doubt he'll want a full update on your investigations."

Elizabeth's brow furrowed as she shared a concerned look with Meli. "Does he often inquire about the investigation, Aunt?"

"It's the first question he asks every time he visits." Aunt Beatrice picked up her teacup, her tone matter of fact.

Elizabeth's voice carried a note of worry. "And how much do you tell him?"

"Only what you've told me, of course." Aunt Beatrice waved a dismissive hand.

Elizabeth paused, considering the extent of the information Aunt Beatrice might have unwittingly shared. "Aunt, please don't share any more information with Mr Gray."

Aunt Beatrice drew herself up, her spine stiffening. "I have nothing to hide, Elizabeth."

Elizabeth's voice softened. "It's not about hiding, Aunt. Sharing information could jeopardise the police investigation. Please, don't tell him anything else."

Aunt Beatrice nodded her ascent, her lips pursing. "Very well." She paused, her gaze settling on Elizabeth. "Although, if you ask me, it seems a great deal of fuss over a bit of chitter chatter."

Elizabeth stood, smoothing her skirt. "We should be off, Aunt. We'll return as soon as we can."

Meli rose. "I'll fetch the pain—"

Elizabeth shook her head, her eyes imploring her not to say anymore. It wasn't that she didn't trust her aunt not to mention the painting to Mr Gray, but she worried that it may slip out in an unguarded moment.

"My … hat," Meli continued, before making her way to the bedroom to retrieve the painting.

Minutes later, they were in the lift, the painting tucked under Meli's coat.

As they crossed the reception area, Elizabeth half expected to see Monsieur Marchand striding towards her, his usual impeccable manners and appearance a stark contrast to the dishevelled form led away in handcuffs the previous evening.

Detective Lefèvre's parting words echoed in her mind. The hotel manager's arrest was linked to the jewellery counterfeiting operation, but the possibility of his involvement in the murder remained. Only time would tell, the detective had said, his tone grave.

Elizabeth and Meli stepped onto the bustling Boulevard de la Croisette, the early morning stillness giving way to the hum of awakening Cannes. A taxi waited, engine purring.

Elizabeth slid into the back seat, Meli close behind. She leaned forward, her voice tight. "Police station, *s'il vous plaît*."

As they navigated the winding streets, Alexander's face flashed in Elizabeth's mind. She blinked hard, refocusing. Clara's testimony had brought them so close, but Detective Lefèvre was right. There was no way Chief Inspector Dubois would take the word of what he would undoubtedly call a love-struck woman. With the chief inspector due back from Marseilles any time, their window to find the actual murderer was shrinking by the hour.

At the station, Detective Lefèvre greeted them, fatigue etched across his face. His gaze softened as it moved from Elizabeth to Meli. "Bonjour, Lady Elizabeth. Mademoiselle Diomaros."

They trailed Detective Lefèvre down the corridor, his hushed conversation with another officer drifting back to them.

Meli leaned close. "Poor man looks like he hasn't slept a wink."

Elizabeth nodded. "Monsieur Marchand's arrest, perhaps?"

The interview room door swung open, revealing Monsieur Bouchér. Elizabeth's breath caught. The polished art broker had vanished, replaced by a dishevelled man, his stained, rumpled clothes and unkempt appearance telling the story of his time on the run and a night in the police cells.

Sympathy clenched Elizabeth's heart. If one night did this to Monsieur Bouchér, what had *La Maison d'Arrêt de Cannes* done to Alexander? She steeled herself. Every second counted now.

Detective Lefèvre cut straight to the chase. "Monsieur Bouchér, your presence in Madame Voss's apartment?"

Bouchér's eyebrow twitched. "I'm afraid you're mistaken, Detective."

"We have a witness." Detective Lefèvre's chair scraped as he leaned forward.

"They're lying." A ghost of Monsieur Bouchér's usual swagger crept into his voice.

Detective Lefèvre produced a small bag, extracting a ring that glinted under the harsh light. He slid it towards Elizabeth. "Lady Elizabeth, do you recognise this ring?"

Elizabeth picked up the ring for a closer look. "Yes, I saw it on the intruder's pinky just before he leapt from the window. I'm certain."

Bouchér's eyes darted nervously around the room before settling on Detective Lefèvre. He drew a deep breath, his shoulders squaring "I used to be an art forger," he admitted, his voice quiet but clear. "One of the best, unfortunately." A rueful smile tugged at his lips. "I met Rene when we both lived in Paris, but by then, I'd reinvented myself as an art dealer, believing I'd left my past behind."

Elizabeth leaned forward, her interest piqued. "So what happened?"

Bouchér's voice grew strained. "When she found out about my past, she blackmailed me into helping her with her jewellery swindle. I was to create fake provenance documents for her counterfeit pieces, make them seem authentic."

Detective Lefèvre's eyes narrowed. "And Marchand? What was his role in all this?"

Bouchér laughed. "Marchand? He was a nobody. Rene used him to gain access to the jewellery in the hotel safe. In return, she gave him a small share of the profits."

"But the painting," Elizabeth pressed, unrolling the painting on the table. "How does it fit into all this?"

Bouchér's gaze fell to the painting, regret and resignation etched on his face. "This was meant to be my last job. Rene claimed she had a buyer – someone discreet but willing to pay handsomely. She promised if I completed this one last task, I'd be free from her blackmail."

"Who?" Meli asked, her voice sharp. "Who was the buyer?"

Bouchér shook his head, his eyes downcast. "I don't know. She never told me... I'm not even sure there was a buyer. I kept my end of the deal, but Rene..."

His voice trailed off, the weight of his choices hanging heavy in the air.

"Then what?" Elizabeth prompted.

Bouchér's shoulders sagged. "She claimed the deal had fallen through. We had to continue as before. She said someone was pressuring her, that she needed more money. But the more she made, the more she craved." He shook his head. "Soon, the counterfeit jewellery wasn't enough. She began keeping the genuine pieces, wearing them in public, flaunting them. She was becoming increasingly reckless."

Detective Lefèvre leaned forward, his voice sharp. "Is that why you murdered her? To protect your new life?"

"I didn't murder her," Monsieur Bouchér protested, his voice rising. "I just... I just wanted it all to end."

"And murder was your solution?" Detective Lefèvre pressed.

"No!" Monsieur Bouchér slammed his fist on the table. The officer by the door tensed, but Detective Lefèvre held up a hand, staying him.

Elizabeth frowned, recalling a previous incident. "The day before Madame Voss died, did you have an altercation with her in the marketplace near *Rue de Rivoli*?"

Bouchér flicked his wrist dismissively. "It was nothing. I'd gone to her apartment to ask for the painting back."

"It didn't look like nothing," Meli interjected. "Madame Voss seemed quite shaken afterwards."

"Madame Voss," Monsieur Bouchér sneered, "appeared to be many things, in case you hadn't noticed."

Elizabeth had to concede his point. Doreen Voss, or whatever her real name was, had played the part of a princess rather convincingly.

Detective Lefèvre leaned back in his chair, his gaze fixed on Monsieur Bouchér. "Where were you between one and two o'clock on the morning of Madame Voss's murder?"

Bouchér's eyes widened slightly. "I was with Marchand. We were meeting a potential buyer, working on some fake provenance certificates for a collection Rene had lined up."

"Can Monsieur Marchand corroborate this?" Detective Lefèvre asked, his tone neutral.

"Yes, of course," Monsieur Bouchér replied, a flicker of relief crossing his face.

Detective Lefèvre nodded, but his expression remained stern. "Even if Monsieur Marchand confirms your alibi, you're still in considerable trouble, Monsieur Bouchér. Your involvement in this counterfeiting operation is a serious matter."

The brief spark of hope in Monsieur Bouchér's eyes dimmed. He slumped in his chair, the weight of his situation visibly settling on his shoulders.

Detective Lefèvre gestured to the officer by the door. "*Ramenez-le dans sa cellule.*"

As the officer led Monsieur Bouchér away, Elizabeth watched him go, her mind already racing with this new information and its implications for their investigation.

As the echo of Monsieur Bouchér's footsteps faded, a heavy silence settled over the room. Elizabeth's gaze darted between Detective Lefèvre and Meli, both lost in thought.

Detective Lefèvre broke the quiet first, his voice low. "A man of many faces, our Monsieur Bouchér."

"Skilled at reinvention," Elizabeth mused, "but does that make him a murderer?"

Meli leaned forward, her eyes bright. "He definitely had motive. If Doreen was threatening his new life..."

"Perhaps," Detective Lefèvre conceded, "but motive isn't everything. We need more."

Elizabeth nodded slowly. "His alibi … It's convenient, isn't it?"

"Too convenient," Detective Lefèvre agreed. "We'll see what Monsieur Marchand has to say. If their stories align..."

"...it could mean they've coordinated their lies," Meli finished.

"Or," Elizabeth added, "it could mean they're telling the truth."

Detective Lefèvre's lips quirked in a half smile. "Indeed. Either way, Marchand's interview should prove ... illuminating."

A sharp rap on the door cut through their discussion. An officer burst in, his face flushed, eyes wide. He beckoned urgently to Detective Lefèvre.

Detective Lefèvre sprang to his feet, his chair scraping against the floor. "Excuse me," he muttered, following the officer out.

The sudden flurry of activity beyond the door set Elizabeth on edge. She exchanged a worried glance with Meli, both straining to catch snippets of the hurried conversations outside.

When Detective Lefèvre strode back in, his jaw was set, eyes blazing with a mix of frustration and determination. "We have to postpone Marchand's interview for now. Monsieur Spencer Roland's just arrived in Paris. He claims Gray is one of the private detectives he hired to find Madame Voss."

Elizabeth's fingers tightened on the arm of her chair. "Mr Gray's a detective? He never said a word about that."

Detective Lefèvre's lips thinned into a hard line. "No, he didn't. Monsieur Roland became suspicious when Gray's reports became irregular and he kept insisting he couldn't find a trace of Madame Voss."

As Detective Lefèvre detailed Monsieur Roland's discoveries – Gray's abandoned office and flat, his claims to his landlady that he'd come into some money – Elizabeth felt her stomach twist into knots.

Meli leaned forward, tension evident in her posture. "What are you going to do?"

"We're bringing Gray in." Detective Lefèvre's tone left no room for argument. "Monsieur Roland and my superior are travelling to Cannes to identify him and formally identify Madame Voss – as far as anyone knows, he's her next of kin."

The blood drained from Elizabeth's face. "Mr Gray was meant to play backgammon with Aunt Beatrice this afternoon."

Detective Lefèvre's eyes flashed with alarm. "Call your aunt. Now. Tell her to cancel. We don't want to take any chances."

Elizabeth reached for the telephone, her mind racing. Gray's slip about Caruso, his intimate knowledge of the princess's cocktail, his boasts about reading people… The pieces were falling into place with alarming speed.

Meli moved closer as Elizabeth waited for the call to connect.

"Lady Hawthorne's suite," Evelyn answered.

Elizabeth straightened. "Evelyn, it's Lady Elizabeth. Is Mr Gray there?"

"No, Lady Elizabeth." A momentary relief washed over Elizabeth, only to be swept away by Evelyn's next words. "Mr Gray took Lady Hawthorne out on his boat. He said the fresh air would do her good and assured her they'd be away from prying eyes."

Elizabeth's fingers tightened on the receiver. "When did they leave?"

"About half an hour ago, my lady."

As Elizabeth replaced the receiver, the horrifying truth crashed over her. Aunt Beatrice's offhand comment about Gray at Barnum and Bailey's – if he'd been an acrobat, that trellis would've been nothing to him.

She whirled to face Detective Lefèvre, her voice tight with barely contained panic. "Mr Gray has taken Aunt Beatrice out … on his boat."

The room fell silent, the weight of realisation settling like lead. Mr Gray was the murderer – and Aunt Beatrice was alone with him on the open water.

Chapter Twenty-One

ELIZABETH'S BLOOD RAN COLD, a chill of dread gripping her heart. Meli's eyes went wide, her face paling with horror. They whirled to face Detective Lefèvre, the detective already springing into action.

Detective Lefèvre's voice cut through the chaos. "Alert the Coast Guard and the marina immediately." He strode towards the door, already reaching for his coat. "Gray's out there with Lady Hawthorne, and we need to find them now."

Without a moment's hesitation, Elizabeth snatched her coat, the fabric rustling with her hurried movements. "We're coming with you," she declared, her voice taut with determination.

Meli was at her side in an instant, brow creased with worry. "There's no time to waste."

The trio burst from the interview room, leaving a flurry of activity in their wake. Elizabeth and Meli raced after Detective Lefèvre, their footsteps echoing against the tiled walls as they navigated the labyrinth of the police station.

They pushed through the doors onto Cannes' bustling streets. The early morning stillness had given way to the hum of awakening life – the chatter of passersby, the rumble of motorcar engines, the clip-clop of horses' hooves. Detective Lefèvre ushered them towards a waiting car, its impatient engine idling.

Elizabeth's fingers trembled as she gripped the door handle, knuckles turning white. Aunt Beatrice was in grave danger, and the weight of it threatened to overwhelm her. As the vehicle lurched forward, scattering gravel in its wake, she willed herself to focus. They had to reach the marina, had to find Aunt Beatrice in time. The alternative was unthinkable.

The motorcar careened through the streets of Cannes, its powerful engine roaring as it wove between startled pedestrians and other vehicles. Elizabeth's fingers dug into the leather seat, her heart pounding in rhythm with the machine's thunderous pistons. The wind whipped through the open windows, stinging her eyes and stealing her breath, but she refused to look away, her gaze fixed on the road ahead.

Within minutes, the bustling Cannes marina materialised before them, a forest of masts swaying against the morning sky. Fishing boats and small craft bobbed on the waves, their hulls creaking in the gentle swell. Detective Lefèvre brought the motorcar to a screeching halt, the tires leaving dark streaks on the cobblestones.

"This way!" he shouted, already sprinting towards the water's edge.

Elizabeth and Meli leapt from the car, their skirts billowing behind them as they raced after the detective. The salty tang of the sea filled Elizabeth's nostrils, mingling with the acrid scent of fish and tar. The gentle lapping of waves against the hulls provided a constant backdrop to their desperate search, a stark contrast to the urgency that propelled them forward.

As they reached the docks, Elizabeth's eyes darted from boat to boat, searching for any sign of Gray or Aunt Beatrice. The enormity of their task struck her – finding one small craft amidst this nautical maze seemed almost impossible. But they had to try. Aunt Beatrice's life depended on it.

The marina assaulted her senses as soon as they arrived – the creak of wood against wood, the snap of canvas sails in the breeze, the shouts of dockhands echoing across the water. Elizabeth's gaze darted from vessel to vessel, her heart pounding with each passing second.

Detective Lefèvre's shoes clacked against the wooden dock as he raced towards a cluster of harbour police. Their rapid-fire French was lost in the cacophony of the marina, but Elizabeth didn't need to understand the words to read the tension in Detective Lefèvre's shoulders, the deepening furrow of his brow.

He turned back to them, his jaw clenched as he raked his fingers through his hair. "A small pleasure yacht vanished from the marina fifteen minutes ago."

Elizabeth's breath caught in her throat. "It must be them. Where—"

"The Lérins Islands," Detective Lefèvre cut in, gesturing towards the distant horizon. He started moving, motioning for the others to follow. "This way."

They raced down the dock, dodging coils of rope and stacks of crates. The police launch bobbed at the end, sleek and powerful. As they clambered aboard, the engine roared to life, vibrating through the deck beneath their feet.

Elizabeth's fingers curled around the railing as they surged forward, spray flying. The wind tore at her hair, salt stinging her eyes, but she refused to look away from the horizon.

Meli's fingers dug into Elizabeth's arm, her knuckles white. "Do you see them?" The wind whipped her words away, making them barely audible over the thunderous rumble of the engine.

Elizabeth squinted against the glare, her eyes scanning the open water. The vastness of the sea stretched before them, a canvas of blue dotted with distant specks. A glint of sunlight on polished brass caught her eye. Her heart leapt. She thrust her arm out, pointing. "There!"

Detective Lefèvre leaned forward, his body tense as a coiled spring. His eyes narrowed, focusing on the distant boat. He twisted towards the harbour police officer at the helm, his voice sharp and urgent. The officer's jaw clenched as he nodded, his hands tightening on the wheel as he gunned the engine.

The police launch surged forward, spray flying as it cut through the waves. Elizabeth gripped the railing, her knuckles white, willing the boat to go faster. She could see the stolen yacht more clearly now, bobbing and weaving as it fled.

The distance between them shrank, metre by metre. Elizabeth's heart pounded in her ears, her silent prayer for Aunt Beatrice's safety lost in the wind.

Without warning, the yacht veered sharply, cutting across their path. The harbour police officer at the helm muttered a curse, his knuckles whitening as he wrenched the wheel around. The launch heeled over, saltwater sluicing across the deck.

Elizabeth stumbled, grabbing onto Meli for support. The yacht darted ahead, weaving between the larger vessels with unnerving agility.

Meli's face drained of colour, her eyes wide. "We're losing them!"

Detective Lefèvre's jaw clenched, a muscle twitching beneath the skin. He leaned in close to the officer, their heads almost touching as they conferred. The officer nodded, his hands moving over the controls. The engine's roar deepened, the deck vibrating beneath their feet as the launch surged forward with renewed power.

Elizabeth braced herself against the railing, her eyes fixed on the fleeing yacht. They were gaining again, the gap closing.

The police launch closed in on the yacht, the gap narrowing with each passing second. Elizabeth's heart pounded as she watched Detective Lefèvre tense, ready to spring.

Without warning, Detective Lefèvre leapt, his body arcing through the air. He landed on the yacht's deck with a thud, immediately lunging for Gray. The two men collided, grappling fiercely.

Detective Lefèvre's fist connected with Gray's jaw, but Gray retaliated, driving his knee into the detective's stomach. They stumbled, locked together, careening towards the starboard railing.

A harbour police officer followed Detective Lefèvre's lead, jumping aboard and rushing to the helm. The yacht's speed dropped as he took control.

Elizabeth kicked off her shoes, knowing they'd only hinder her. She gripped the railing, waiting for the right moment.

As the yacht slowed, the police launch drew alongside. Elizabeth didn't hesitate. She leapt across, her stocking feet sliding as she landed on the deck. She caught herself on a nearby seat, steadying herself against the yacht's motion.

"Aunt Beatrice!" Elizabeth's eyes darted across the yacht, searching frantically.

Near the bow, her aunt sat, looking remarkably composed despite the chaos around her. Elizabeth rushed to her side, relief flooding through her.

She knelt beside Aunt Beatrice, her hands hovering uncertainly. "Are you all right?"

Aunt Beatrice sniffed, reaching up to adjust her hat. "My dear Elizabeth, after surviving the loss of your uncle and cousin, and those dreadful years of war, this little misadventure is hardly worth mentioning."

Behind them, a thud and a grunt signalled Detective Lefèvre gaining the upper hand. Elizabeth glanced back to see Gray pinned face-down on the deck. The harbour police officer stepped forward, handcuffs glinting in the sunlight. The click of metal punctuated Gray's defeat.

Elizabeth grasped her aunt's arm, helping her to her feet. They made their way towards the stern, where the police launch bobbed alongside. Aunt Beatrice patted her niece's hand.

A wry smile played at the corners of her mouth. "I do hope this kidnapping business won't become a habit. It's dreadfully inconvenient and so terribly uncivilised."

Chapter Twenty-Two

ELIZABETH CLOSED THE LID OF her trunk with a soft thud. Their holiday, which had begun as a simple escape from the dreary English winter, had transformed into an adventure none of them could have anticipated.

As she straightened up, her thoughts turned to Alexander. His ordeal was over, the false accusations dispelled, and his reputation intact. With Clara by his side, he seemed a changed man – lighter, more at ease with himself. Their engagement, announced just yesterday, had been met with genuine joy from both families.

"It's a love match, to be sure," Aunt Beatrice had remarked, a hint of approval in her voice. "And if Miss Hicks's considerable fortune helps restore Wexford to its former glory, well, that's a most fortuitous stroke of fate."

Elizabeth smiled at the memory. Aunt Beatrice had surprised them all with her growing fondness for Clara, despite her initial reservations about the young American's suitability. Mrs Hicks, on the other hand, remained a formidable sparring partner for Aunt Beatrice, their verbal jousts a source of both exasperation and amusement for the rest of the family.

Meli emerged from the bathroom, her eyes bright with excitement. "Are you ready?" she asked, practically bouncing on her toes. "I can't believe it's time to leave already."

Elizabeth nodded, casting one last glance around the room. "It seems like only yesterday we arrived," she mused. "So much has happened."

Her mind drifted to Detective Lefèvre's final report, delivered just yesterday. The ashtray they'd uncovered in the garden had indeed been confirmed as the murder weapon. Despite the rain and burial compromising much of the evidence, the coroner had even ventured that the fatal blow was likely struck by a right-handed person. Elizabeth felt a surge of vindication; that detail alone would have exonerated the left-handed Alexander, had Mr Gray not been exposed as the actual murderer. It was a bittersweet confirmation of their early suspicions, arriving too late to make a difference in the case, yet somehow satisfying nonetheless.

Meli's expression sobered slightly. "I still can't believe Mr Gray turned out to be the murderer. To think he scaled that trellis and lay in wait for the princess—or rather, Madame Voss."

"At least justice has been served," Elizabeth replied. "And not just for the princess. Monsieur Marchand and Monsieur Bouchér will face the consequences of their part in that dreadful counterfeiting scheme."

"True," Meli agreed. "Though I feel for those poor souls left with nothing but paste imitations of their jewellery."

As they made their way downstairs, Evelyn approached them, her arms laden with Aunt Beatrice's hatboxes. "Lady Beatrice is waiting for you in the lobby," she informed them with a smile. "She's been having quite the catch-up with Monsieur Gaston."

They found Aunt Beatrice engaged in what appeared to be a pleasant exchange with the hotel manager.

"Ah, there you are," Beatrice said, turning to greet them. "I was just telling Monsieur Gaston how pleased I am to see him back in his rightful place as manager. Le Majestique is in much better hands now, I'm sure."

Elizabeth couldn't help but notice the spring in her aunt's step, the way she held her head high. The ordeal with Mr Gray had shaken Aunt Beatrice more than she'd admit, but she had emerged from it with her indomitable spirit intact. No doubt contributing to her aunt's improved mood was the news Elizabeth had shared earlier that morning. Thanks to the swift resolution of the case and some discreet manoeuvring by Detective Lefèvre, Cybil Hughes had assured Elizabeth that Alexander's brief incarceration had never made it into the British press. His name had been cleared before any whisper of scandal had reached the English Channel. The thought of returning to England without the spectre of gossip hanging over them had lightened Aunt Beatrice's heart.

As they stepped out onto the promenade, Elizabeth spotted Alexander and Clara bidding farewell to Monsieur Renault. The jeweller had been instrumental in helping Alexander recover the parure and halt the sale of the Sargent painting, ensuring they were returned to their rightful place at the Wexford estate.

"I do hope you'll visit us in Wexford, Monsieur Renault," Clara was saying, her hand tucked into the crook of Alexander's arm. "We'd be delighted to have you."

Elizabeth thought back to the previous evening's dinner at La Rotunda. Detective Lefèvre had been a charming companion, and she couldn't help but notice how attentive he'd been to Meli. It was a shame he'd been called back to Paris so soon.

"I hear Chief Inspector Dubois has taken early retirement," Aunt Beatrice remarked as they climbed into the waiting motorcar. "Though whether it was entirely his choice is another matter."

Elizabeth settled into her seat as Victor pulled away from the front of Le Majestique, her gaze drifting to the Riviera coastline as it slipped past the motorcar's window. The events of the past weeks played through her mind – a whirlwind of danger, intrigue, and unexpected alliances.

A wry smile tugged at her lips. Who would have thought their winter escape would turn into such an escapade?

The motorcar rounded a bend, and Le Majestique vanished from view. Elizabeth turned her attention to the road ahead, to England and home. Their time in Cannes had been extraordinary, but she found herself looking forward to the familiar comforts of home.

As Aunt Beatrice discussed plans for Alexander and Clara's engagement party, Elizabeth allowed her thoughts to wander. What fresh adventures might be waiting for them back in England?

Only time would tell.

Epilogue

ELIZABETH SETTLED INTO THE drawing-room sofa at Hawthorne House, the evening edition of The Times spread across her lap. Two weeks had passed since their return from Cannes, the Riviera adventure now a distant memory. Mafdet, her Abyssinian cat, lounged on the cushion beside her, a respectable distance away as befitted her regal status. The cat's ruddy fur gleamed in the lamplight, her tail occasionally twitching in silent judgment of the world around her.

Mafdet's golden eyes, half-lidded with boredom, surveyed the room with thinly veiled contempt. When Elizabeth's hand reached to stroke her, the cat arched away, clearly affronted by the unsolicited attention. She repositioned herself, turning her back to Elizabeth in a clear display of feline superiority.

Across the room, Meli crouched on the Persian rug, her brow furrowed in concentration. "Winston, sit."

The young mongrel's ears perked up, one floppy and one pointed, at the sound of his name. His tail thumped against the rug, but his bottom remained off the ground.

Meli's fingers curled into the plush carpet. "Winston…"

The pup cocked his head, brown eyes wide with feigned innocence. He inched forward, pink tongue darting out to lick Meli's hand.

A stray curl fell across Meli's forehead as she shook her head, lips twitching. "You're impossible … if only you weren't so adorable…"

Winston flopped onto his back, paws waving in the air. His whole body wriggled, a furry display of shameless manipulation.

Meli's resolve crumbled. She reached out, scratching the pup's exposed belly. "How did such a tiny thing get to be so crafty, hmm?"

Winston's leg kicked in delight, his size belying the strength of his hold on Meli's affections.

For a moment, the failed training session was forgotten, replaced by the simple joy of a girl and her dog.

Elizabeth chuckled, shaking her head at Meli and Winston's antics. Her gaze drifted back to the newspaper, scanning the columns until—.

She blinked. Read the line again.

The paper crinkled as Elizabeth leaned forward, elbows on her knees.

Mafdet's tail twitched. The Abyssinian's ears flattened at Winston's excited bark. She fixed the playful pup with a withering stare, then closed her eyes, determined to ignore the undignified display.

Elizabeth lowered the newspaper and turned to her sister-in-law. "Caroline, you won't believe this. Alfie Tanner is riding in the Grand National."

Caroline's book slipped from her grasp, landing with a soft thud on the carpet. "Alfie Tanner?"

"The very same," Elizabeth said. "The article praises his equine skill. It seems he's made quite a name for himself in racing circles."

Caroline leaned forward, her novel sliding unnoticed to the floor. "How extraordinary. Who would have thought little Alfie would make it to Aintree?"

Meli paused her play with Winston, curiosity piqued. "Who's Alfie?"

"His family has worked in the stables at Hawthorne Hall for generations," Elizabeth explained. "And now he's competing in one of the most prestigious horse races in the world."

Caroline's fingers drummed against the arm of her chair. "We should attend. I'm sure William would be interested to see how Alfie has fared."

Elizabeth's eyes lit up. "It would be quite something to witness, wouldn't it? We could plan a trip – take the train up, perhaps book rooms at the Royal Hotel..."

As they discussed the possibilities, Winston trotted over to Elizabeth, his tail swinging like a metronome. Mafdet's ears flattened against her head. She rose, stretching languidly, her claws extending into the sofa cushion. With a flick of her tail, she leapt to the floor. Pausing at the doorway, she cast a last, withering glance at the excited dog, her whiskers twitching. Then, with slow, deliberate steps, she sauntered from the room, her head held high.

Curious about the real Doreen Voss behind the aristocratic façade of Princess Sofia? Join my newsletter for an exclusive bonus scene!

https://dl.bookfunnel.com/xbks7uwrt6

If you enjoyed **'Murder on the French Riviera',** then check out Book 4 in the Lady Elizabeth Hawthorne Mystery series, **'Murder at the Grand National'**

Horses, high stakes, and a homicide at the hurdles.

When tragedy strikes at the 1924 Grand National, Lady Elizabeth Hawthorne gallops headlong into a deadly game of cat and mouse. With the enigmatic Jonathan Ashcroft's loyalties in question and sin-

ister forces conspiring against her, Elizabeth must outrun a killer to expose the truth. As danger lurks at every turn, will her relentless pursuit of justice lead to a photo finish, or will she fall at the final hurdle?

Pre-order your copy now :
https://books2read.com/u/mByeyA

Newsletter

Join my Newsletter to receive your FREE copy of Shadow of the Desert Queen, and keep up to date with all the news about new releases, giveaways, promotions, etc.

https://dl.bookfunnel.com/1x00ah4bcx

Dedication

For my crazy, funny, mad, full-on family, who drive me nuts, mostly.
But I wouldn't have it any other way.
xxx

Also by Olivia Rose

MURDER ON THE SS ANDROMEDA

Champagne, caviar, and a side of murder.

When death crashes the party aboard the luxurious SS Andromeda, Lady Elizabeth Hawthorne's mission to escort a priceless Greek artifact to London takes a sinister turn. The captain's mysterious demise plunges Elizabeth into a deadly game of cat and mouse, where every passenger is a suspect and every smile could mask murderous intent.

Teaming up with lifelong alley, Major Sinclair, Elizabeth dives into a labyrinth of secrets and lies. As they navigate clandestine soirees and whispered conspiracies, the line between ally and adversary blurs. With each uncovered clue, the danger mounts, and trust becomes as fragile as crystal stemware.

Racing against time and a killer's cunning, Elizabeth and Major Sinclair must unravel the twisted web of deceit before the Andromeda docks in Liverpool. But in this floating world of glittering facades and hidden agendas, one misstep could turn their investigation deadly.

Can Elizabeth unmask the murderer lurking among the elite, or will she become the next victim in this high-stakes game of death on the high seas?

https://books2read.com/u/bpnBjX

MURDER AT MAYFIELD MANOR

Blackmail, betrayal and a body in the bath.

Lady Elizabeth Hawthorne's joyous reunion with childhood friend Clemmi Mayfield takes a sinister turn when she uncovers a chilling web of secrets: a hidden marriage, vicious blackmail, and the Countess Magdalena von Habsfeld dead in her bath.

As a relentless blizzard seals the manor, trapping guests and their dark pasts within its frozen walls, suspicion falls on everyone – including Clemmi herself.

Once again thrust into an uneasy alliance with the enigmatic Jonathan Ashcroft, Elizabeth plunges into a labyrinth of decades-old secrets and fresh betrayals. With each revelation, the danger mounts, and she realizes that in this house of lies, even her closest friend could be a deadly enemy.

Racing against both the clock and the elements, Elizabeth must unravel the twisted threads of deceit before the killer strikes again.

But in this snow-bound manor of secrets and shadows, can Elizabeth unmask the killer before she becomes the final victim?

https://books2read.com/u/mlMzDA

MURDER AT THE GRAND NATIONAL

Horses, high stakes, and a homicide at the hurdles.

When the 1924 Grand National ends in tragedy, Lady Elizabeth Hawthorne finds herself embroiled in a deadly conspiracy that reaches far beyond the racetrack.

As the dust settles on Aintree's hallowed turf, celebrated jockey Reggie Blackwood lies dead, and Alfie – a former stable boy from Hawthorne Hall – stands accused of murder. Convinced of Alfie's innocence, Elizabeth is determined to uncover the truth.

With a Chief Inspector eager to close the case and the enigmatic Jonathan Ashcroft, whose true motives grow increasingly suspect with each encounter, Elizabeth must navigate a treacherous course. Every step brings her closer to a truth that powerful forces want buried – and puts her squarely in the crosshairs of a killer who'll stop at nothing to keep their secrets.

In a world where fortunes are won and lost on the turn of a hoof, Elizabeth is about to discover that the deadliest wagers are made far from the finish line. Can she unmask the true culprit before the killer strikes again, or will her pursuit of justice lead her to a fate worse than Becher's Brook?

https://books2read.com/u/4A19JN

About the Author

Born and raised in Wales, Olivia and her husband relocated to the Mediterranean island of Cyprus twenty years ago with their two children.

Sharing their home with five cats, two dogs, and a small colony of indigenous creepy crawlies means life is never dull.

Olivia's new series, Lady Elizabeth Hawthorne Mysteries, transports readers back in time to the vibrant and sophisticated world of 1920s England through the captivating tales of Lady Elizabeth Hawthorne. The daughter of an English lord and a Grecian adventuress, Elizabeth's lineage is as rich as the mysteries she uncovers. Her innate passion for archaeology, a legacy from her parents, propels her into a realm filled with ancient secrets and high-society intrigue.

Made in the USA
Coppell, TX
12 January 2025